Teenage
Bluez

Published by
Life Changing Books
P.O. Box 423
Brandywine, MD 20613
www.lifechangingbooks.net

Life Changing Books and the portrayal of a person reading are trademarks of Life Changing Books.

ISBN: 0-9741394-9-1

Cover design: OCJ Graphix/Kevin Carr
Book design: Holscher Type & Design/Brian Holscher

This book is a work of fiction. Names, characters, places and incidents are products of the author's imagination or are used fictitiously. Any resemblance to actual events or locales or persons, living or dead, is entirely coincidental.

Printed in the United States of America

3 6645 00041987 9

Acknowledgements

The authors of Teenage Bluez would like to give thanks to God for guiding our hands and thoughts to write these stories. Prayerfully these stories will help teenagers from all over the world who have or are experiencing similar situations.

We would also like to thank our parents, who gave us the encouragement when we needed it the most. To our friends, you all know who you are, we say thank you!!

To the technical support, Kevin Carr, thanks for designing such an eye catching cover. Thanks to the book cover model, Courtney Kinney. Kathleen Jackson, our Project Coordinator, thanks for all of your help and work.

TEENAGE
BLUEZ
SERIES 1

Table of Contents

LIVIN' IN THE FAST LANE
by Khadijah Knight

It's now 8 o'clock in the evening, just one hour before the back to school party at Jamel's house was scheduled to start, and here I am still unsure of what to wear. I knew I was going to wear my dark blue Apple Bottom jeans, but I couldn't decide between my black Bob Marley tube top and my pink Vintage belly shirt.

"Ahh, this is so frustrating!" I said to myself, totally aggravated.

It was so hard deciding on the perfect outfit, especially when I'm trying to impress a guy that doesn't even know I exist. That guy is Jamel Watkins.

Jamel is a senior at my school and not only is he popular, but he is indeed the finest boy in all of Maryland, or at least out of the ones I've seen. He's 6 feet, with dreads that touch his shoulders, has the smoothest brown skin, and the most perfect body that I've ever seen on a 17-year old boy. Not only does Jamel get an A+ in looks, but he also gets an A+ in smarts. I've heard that he's maintained a 3.0 grade point average since the 9th grade; he has brains and beauty, the full package. Any girl would kill to get next to him, even me.

Anyway, the party was scheduled to start at 9 o'clock, so I really needed to hurry up because it was already 8:15. I decided to call Leah to see what she was wearing because maybe we could coordinate. I picked up my cell phone and dialed Leah's number.

"Hello," Leah's mom said, answering the phone.

"Hi, Mrs. Parker. It's Aerin, is Leah home?" I asked politely.

"Yes she is Aerin. Hold on."

Within seconds, I heard Leah's raspy voice in my ear. "Hello."

"Hey girl, I'm calling to find out what you're wearing to Jamel's party."

As soon as I asked her that, she got really excited. Leah has always been a good dresser. "Girl, I'm wearing my tennis skirt with the Jamaican colors and my black halter top. It's so cute," she said excitedly. "So, what are you wearing?"

"I'm wearing jeans, but I can't decide between my black tube top or my belly shirt. Which one do you think I should wear?"

"You should wear your belly shirt so that Jamel can peek your curves and flat stomach," she said laughing.

"Yeah right. Anyway, are you coming over here or do I have to meet you at your house?"

"Since the bus stop is near your house, I'll come over there. Give me 15 minutes," Leah replied.

"Alright, but it's already 8:40, so hurry up," I said, obviously rushing her.

"Don't rush me, bighead. It's not my fault you called and had me on the phone all this time."

"Alright, jerk. See you in 15," I said, before hanging up.

Leah is my best friend in the whole world and has been since the fifth grade. She's my better half. We're like two peas in a pod, Paris Hilton and Nicole Richie, Ben and Jerry, tight as shoelaces. We're both about the same height and have figures to die for. Leah wears braces, has dark brown hair, and brown skin kissed by the sun. She's like me; she likes partying and just having a lot of fun. We do almost everything together because we both like the same things. But Jus, who is Leah's sister, on the other hand, is totally the opposite.

Jus is tall, wears glasses and has a killer shape, but she doesn't know how to use it and she really doesn't care to find out. She has always been the oddball when it came to hanging out or just all of us doing something together. Our idea of fun is nowhere near hers. Jus is the type of person who always put her education before everything else and she does her own thing, despite what everybody else is doing. That's why we love her, because she's a leader and not a follower. Parties really don't interest her that much, but since this was going to be the mother of all parties, we decided to try and get her to bend a little this time. No such luck, she wasn't interested.

As I was putting the finishing touches on my hair and make-up, I wondered if my mom had any black hoop earrings. I had broken mine at the last party I went to. I didn't even know if she was in the house or not. I decided if she wasn't home, I'd get the earrings and put them back later.

My mom, Michelle Washington, is 33 and she's one of those parents whom you live in the same house with but y'all barely see each other. She was either always working, closed up in her room or out with one of her new boyfriends. We really don't have that mother-daughter bond. No type of communication whatsoever. She really doesn't break her neck saying anything to me except for, "There's food on the stove" or "I'm leaving, if you go out lock up." Half the time, she doesn't even say that, she just leaves.

I can't remember the last time we actually sat down and talked about anything. I mean really had a serious conversation. But it wasn't always this way. It started when I was ten and my dad walked out on us. Ever since then, it's like she has no time for me. But I don't really trip, because I do Aerin regardless of whatever happens.

When I got to her room, I realized she was gone. I couldn't believe that she hadn't said *didley squat*. I hadn't even heard her leave. I went in and grabbed the earrings. I wondered if she was gonna say anything if I came home late, or for that matter, whether she would even be here when I got home. I wasn't going to take that chance, so I decided to stay at Leah's tonight. But I refused to be like her, I was gonna leave her a note and let her know where I was going to be.

I walked back to my room to get my hoody in case it got chilly and got my house keys. I looked at the clock and it read 9:15.

"I know Leah had better hurry up," I said aloud to myself.

DING, DONG! Saved by the doorbell. I walked over to the door and looked out the peephole before opening it.

"Girl, you forever late for somethin'," I said to Leah.

"Sometimes it's good to be fashionably late to a party. That way we can make a grand entrance." The girls slapped hands.

"Yeah, that's true. We'll be the center of attention when Jamel sees how good I look, he'll wanna ask me to dance," I said, with glee.

"Girl, please. He's probably gonna be bunin' up with some other chick by the time we get there," Leah said, crushing the whole moment.

"Stop hatin', there's nothing worse than a hater." I rolled my eyes at her. "What took you so long anyway?" I asked, locking my front door.

"My mom was talking a hole in my head. She was like, 'Now Leah, don't do anything that you wouldn't do around me. No drinking, no smoking and, most of all, no sex!' I had to assure her that I was going to this party just to have fun."

We stepped off my front porch and headed toward the bus stop. Leah was always complaining about her mom nagging her all the time. Mrs. Parker is a little older than most parents. She's 50 and can get a little overprotective at times. Personally, I feel like she has a good relationship with Leah and Jus. They hang out together and they talk about almost everything. For her mom to be so ancient, she's down to earth with the teenage thing. I often wonder what it would be like if my mom and I had that kind of relationship. I tell Leah all the time she shouldn't trip when her mom warns her or asks questions. She's only doing it for her own good.

"At least your mom cares. My mom is never around to tell me anything," I said sadly.

"Girl, all I'm thinking about is the food. I hope they got some serious refreshments cause a sistah gotta eat," Leah said, rubbing her stomach. She knew it was a good time to change the subject.

"You don't go to a party to eat greedy gut. You do that at small get-togethers. At parties, you go to look cute, dance, and look at cute guys," I explained to her.

"Well, that's what you do. Me, I look for good grub."

I rolled my eyes in the back of my head, disturbed by her ignorance. We got to the bus stop and sat down on the bench and continued to talk about the party.

"I hope that Mike will be there," Leah said.

"Who is that?" I asked, really wanting to know.

"That's Jamel's cousin. He used to go to our school, but now he goes to Dupont," she said, trying to refresh my memory.

"Oh, I remember. He's a'ight, but he's not anyone for you to be geekin' off," I said seriously.

"Pleeaasse, he's a bun!"

"Whatever."

The bus pulled up shortly afterwards. I don't know what it was but when I got on the bus, all I kept thinking about was Jamel. No boy has ever been on my mind as much as he has. It's something so special about him and I had to find out what it was.

It was so crowded on the bus that there wasn't even enough space for Leah and me to sit together. I had to sit next to this big, fat, dingy plumber with the name Joe stitched on his work shirt. He smelled so bad that I was dazed for a minute. I felt like I was taken to a whole different planet. As soon as I got my mind back to earth, I laid my head back, held my breath and thought of Jamel the rest of the bus ride.

I was so happy when we finally got off the bus on Turner Avenue, the street Jamel lived on. I checked my watch; it was 10:45. "So much for being fashionably late," I said to Leah.

Jamel lived four houses down from the bus stop on the left hand side. It was the best looking house on the whole block. As we approached the house, we saw that it was decorated with teenagers on the front lawn, either just arriving or coming out of the house to mingle or get some air. Leah and I strutted ourselves up the long driveway as if we were the hottest chicks at the party. I walked up the five stairs that led to the front door, greeting fellow classmates on the way. When I got to the door, I didn't know whether I should knock or go in. Leah sensed my hesitation, and since the door was already ajar, she took it upon herself to just walk in. We were amazed at how nice it was inside. From the looks of the place, we were sure that the Watkins' had mad taste and money because the house was beautiful.

In the corner of the living room was a black Baby Grand Piano, accompanied by a Persian rug to set off the color. Not to mention the crystal chandelier that greeted us on the way in. From the spiral staircase, you could see the 20-seat dining room table and the Hitachi big/flat screen TV. All of this gave me confirmation that the Watkins' were the bomb.

"Now I know that I have to marry this guy. I can definitely

see myself in here. Leah, he's gonna be the one to take me out the ghetto," I said, quite confidently.

"Girl, please, you need to meet him first and let him in on all these plans you have," she said laughing.

"What did I tell you, Leah? Hate doesn't look good on you. Besides, he'll want to meet me tonight when he sees how fly I'm looking."

"Okay, Aerin," she said, really hoping I'd stop dreaming.

We walked into the kitchen and across the marble floor to get to the basement. The closer we got to all the action, the louder the music sounded. I heard Nelly's song, '*Drop Down and Get Your Eagle On*' blaring through the speakers. This had to be one of Leah's songs judging by the way she immediately started dancing and urging me to open the basement door. Going down the basement stairs, we had to hold onto the handrail because there was no light, other than the black and white strobe in the corner of the basement. It made it look like everyone was moving in slow motion, giving the basement a club atmosphere.

When we reached the bottom of the stairs, we saw that in every inch of the basement, there were hot and sweaty teenagers grinding up against one another. The odor in the room was awful!! The smell of marijuana, body spray and musk filled the air. It spelled out straight up *FUNK!* Some of these people had a *serious* case of rawhide and I was here to confirm that perfume doesn't mix with stank. The part that made it worse was the fact that it had to be about 80 degrees and climbing.

Everyone was dressed for the occasion. The girls had on tight shirts, mini skirts, daisy dukes, and halter-tops. The guys had on their usual white or black t-shirts, jeans, wife beaters, and some didn't have on any shirt at all. Everybody had their own little cliques. There was the half naked crew, the I came but I'm not dancing crew, the I came to go buck wild partying crew, and last but not least, the I came to see who was going to be here and who I can hate on crew. I guess Leah and I were a little bit of everything, but since it was only the two of us, we were the crew that all the girls would look at and say, "Eww, look at them, they think they hot."

We looked around trying to find the perfect spot to park ourselves. As I was scanning the crowd, I spotted Jamel with about five girls trying to snatch him up. I figured I'd just forget about trying to catch his eye for right now. He wouldn't have noticed me with all those boobies in his face anyway. I decided that I'd just lay low for a while. Even though Jamel was my main focus, this was still a party and I was gonna have a good time.

Shortly after making that decision, *'Get Busy',* the reggae song by Sean Paul came on and by the way Leah pulled me onto the dance floor, I assumed that was another one of her favorites. I always knew that Leah was a good dancer, but she was a bomb reggae dancer. I wasn't too bad myself. Even though everybody was dancing, it seemed like all eyes were on us. I don't know what it was, but it was like we were hitting all the right moves. I was sure that after this, Jamel was going to notice me because I saw him in the midst of the crowd getting an eye full.

The song ended and everyone was dappin' and givin' us our props. I felt like a superstar. I was tired as I don't know what and needed to get something to drink. On my way over to get a soda, I still had people all on me about the dance thing. Then there were the haters muggin', so all I did was put on my shades to block out all hatin' broads.

When I got to the bar, I felt a huge bump up against my arm. At first I was like, "Oh heck no, I know one of these girls wasn't bold enough to bump me!" I was about to go Shaniqua on one of these broads. But just before I went off, I took a second look and I saw that it was a guy who had bumped me. That was a relief because I was bumped rather hard and any broad that hit that hard, I would've had to fight dirty.

When I looked closely at the guy who had bumped me, I saw that it was the man of my dreams, Jamel. I had a glow on my face that lit up the whole room. I instantly felt like this was my chance to shine for him. My glow soon went dim when I realized that he didn't even look my way. All he did was hold his arm out in a gesture that said, "Oh, my bad." I was so blown away.

After I got my soda, I walked away from the bar to go find Leah because she was the only one that could calm me down. I found her by the staircase getting wrapped up by some B2k, Omarion reject looking brotha. She looked so fascinated talking to this bama, but right now I needed her more than he did. I walked up to her and grabbed her by the arm forcefully.

"What you doin'?" Leah asked, taken aback by my strength.

"I need you. You wouldn't believe what just happened to me. I…" Before I could finish my sentence, the brotha Leah had been talking to cut me off.

"Hey, I was in the middle of something," he said, pissed off that I had interrupted them.

Lord, why did he do that? "Look at my face, does it look like I care?" I gave him a look that if my eyes could kill, he'd be dead. Judging by the way he turned and walked away, he knew I wasn't playing.

"What could have happened to you that was so important that you had to scare that fine brotha away?" Leah asked.

"Jamel bumped into me on my way to the bar and…"

"Oh, that's good. Did you get his number?" Leah asked, cutting me off.

"No, all he said was 'my bad' and walked away," I said sadly.

"Aw, you'll be a'ight, just try again. I have to find that

brotha, Chris, I was talking to." Leah began to walk away until I pulled her back.

"But Leah, what should I do? He might not notice me again."

"Do like I said, try again. Even if it takes you goin' up to him yourself," she said, as she walked away.

I can't do that because I'll just look like all the other girls that's been stepping to him all night, I said to myself. *But if I want him then I have to do what it takes to get him.*

For almost an hour, I watched Jamel talking to girl after girl after girl. I still felt like I had a shot because none of them had anything on me. Not my coca-cola bottle shape, long sandy brown hair, flawless brown skin or my hazel eyes. The only thing that I had to worry about was getting up close and personal with him.

I took a long, deep breath, exhaled and walked toward the spot where Jamel stood. On my way over, I said to myself, *don't screw up, keep cool and don't say anything dumb.* I got about two feet away from him and realized he saw me coming. All of a sudden he got this look on his face like he just saw something he didn't want to see. That changed my whole demeanor. What? Did I have a booger or something? Was a tit hanging out? What was it?

But before I could get to Jamel, I heard a huge bang. I turned to see two dudes rumbling. The loud bang was one of them gettin' thrown up against a table. Jamel and a couple other dudes trampled over me to get to the fight. At that point, all I was thinking was, *can my night get any worse?*

Next thing you know, Jamel was breaking the fight up and throwing people out of his house. I overheard him say, "If you disrespect my house, you disrespect me!" I met up with Leah and we went on our way to her house.

"I can't believe this," Leah said, as we waited at the bus

stop.

"Yeah, but at least you got to talk to Chris. I didn't even get a chance to talk to with Jamel, other then him bumping into me, before the fight broke out," I said.

We rode the after hours bus to Leah's and I was silent the whole way there. I had nothing else to say for the rest of the night.

*   *   *

Another Monday, and the beginning of another school year of me being without a boyfriend, and not just any boy, but my knight in shining armor, Jamel. I was still blown away that a fight had started just when I'd mustered up enough courage to step to him. I wondered if maybe it wasn't meant for me to get with Jamel, or if it just wasn't meant for me to talk to him on that particular night. He probably wouldn't have given me the time of day anyway. What would he want with me, a 15-year old sophomore?

Those were all the things running through my head as I walked toward my locker. I saw Leah racing toward me and she had this look on her face that said, 'You're not gonna believe what I just did.' I braced myself for whatever she was about to say.

"What's up?" I asked her, opening my locker to throw my books in.

"Girl, you know how upset you were Saturday when you didn't get a chance to hook up with Jamel? Well, I…" I cut her off.

"No, Leah, it's okay. I've decided that maybe it just wasn't meant to be. I'm alright," I assured her.

"Well, that's so good. Then I guess I can tell Jamel that you won't be needing this." She held up a piece of paper with his number on it. Leah acted as if she was going to tear it up.

"What? Oh no, wait! How did you get his number?" I asked, in total shock.

"Remember Chris, the guy I was talking to at the party? Well, he's one of Jamel's boys. Today when I was walking to my class Chris called me over and introduced me to Jamel. He remembered me from our reggae dancing. He asked me who that other girl dancin' with me was? And I was like, my best friend, Aerin. He was like, 'Baby girl is fine. I'm gonna try and holla at her.' Then I gave him your number and he gave me his to give to you," Leah said, completely out of breath.

"Are you serious? This can't be real. I knew he was going to be mine," I said, totally excited.

"Girl, I guess he noticed you after all. But do you want his number or what?" Leah asked, acting like she was tired of holding the paper with his number on it.

"Yeah girl, I want his number. I'm gonna call him tonight," I said, putting the number in my purse.

On our way to lunch, I had the biggest smile on my face. I just couldn't stop thanking Leah. That's why she's my best friend; she's always looking out for me. What I thought was going to be a totally screwed day, turned out to be one of the best days of my life.

When I got home from school, I was surprised to see that my mom was home. This was very unusual. I was even more surprised when I came in and she said hello to me.

"Hi, Aerin," she said, when I walked into the living room.

"Uh, hi Ma," I said, rather awkwardly.

I went to my room, changed my clothes, and started on my homework. My mom came to my room and stood in the doorway as if she had something to say, but didn't know how to say it or where to start.

I figured I'd start her off with a simple, "Yes, Ma?"

"Oh nothing. I just wanted to see what you were doing and how your day went," she said, kind of stuttering.

"It was good. I'm just tryna get some homework done right now. How was your day?"

"It was wonderful."

I didn't know if she was having problems with one of her boyfriends or her job, but she seemed really needy today. The talk started to interest me when she asked me about my life and what's been going on with me. After about forty-five minutes of stimulating conversation, she told me she had to go take care of something at her office and that she'd be back later. I was shocked that she had actually told me where she was going this time. I told her that we should talk like this more often and she agreed. I was beginning to believe that, just maybe, our relationship was starting to get better.

When I finished my homework, I went into the kitchen and got something to eat. Since it was 5 o'clock, I went into the den and turned on Maury Povich. That show always makes me laugh every time I watch it. It's basically always about stupid girls that open their legs to different guys, and then they have to come on the show to get various guys tested because they don't know who their baby daddy is. How can someone go on national television and broadcast all of their business to the whole world?

As I was watching the show, I felt myself getting sleepy. It never fails, everyday I come home from school and get sleepy. I try to fight it because when I go to sleep during the day, then I can't sleep at night. But after a while, my eyes got too heavy and I couldn't fight it anymore. The next thing I knew, I was dead asleep on my beanbag chair.

When I woke up it was 9 o'clock at night. I stretched and rolled over to pick up the phone to call Leah. As I went to pick it up, I saw the paper with Jamel's number sitting beside the phone. I remembered that earlier I had taken it out of my bag. I had been trying to get up the nerve to call him.

I immediately changed my mind about calling Leah. As I was dialing Jamel's number, I felt the butterflies in my stomach fluttering as if they were about to come out of my mouth.

The phone rang three times and then I heard his sweet, sexy voice say, "Hello."

My heart stopped. It seemed as if I couldn't speak. He had to say hello two more times before I could say anything.

"Uh, hello, is this Jamel?" I asked, knowing good and well it was.

"Yeah, who is this?"

"My name is Aerin. My friend, Leah, gave you my number today. I was one of the girls that was reggae dancing at your party."

"Oh yeah, I remember. How you doing sweetheart?"

"I'm good. What's up with you?"

"I'm chillin' as usual. So, your girl say you been tryna get with me for the longest." *Thanks a lot Leah.*

"I've seen you around, but it wasn't anything serious." I was so lying right now.

"Oh, okay. Well, I was really feeling you at the party. I saw you looking, why didn't you scoop me up?"

"Well, if you were feeling me, why didn't you step to me? And, considering all the other females you had all up in your grill, I thought you were already taken."

"Yeah, by you," he said, in a real sexy voice.

"Oh, really?" I asked, knowing that was game, but I really didn't care.

"Yeah, so what you think about me snatchin' you up?" he said.

"Well, it depends on whether or not you have what it takes to snatch me up," I said, tryna play hard to get.

"Trust me, I got it and some more, boo." After I heard him call me boo, I almost melted like a popsicle on a hot summer day.

"Well, I have to figure out what to do with my boyfriend," I said, still tryna play hard to get.

"I know you don't have one, but you're 'bout to."

"How do you know I don't have a boyfriend Mr. Jamel?" I asked.

"Cause I'm gonna be your boyfriend."

We talked for about two hours, getting to know one another. Before hanging up, we agreed to meet for lunch tomorrow. When we finished talking, I called and woke Leah up. We stayed up all night talking about Jamel and Chris. All of my dreams were finally coming true.

Jamel and I have been inseparable. Every time I think of him or mention his name, it puts a smile on my face. We spend mostly all of our time together going to the movies, the mall, or out to eat. I used to be a hopeless girl in love with a guy that didn't even know I existed. I was on the outside looking in. Now that I'm all up in the house, I know that Jamel has the full package. He knows exactly what to say and when to say it. He spends money on me and let's me know that I'm his woman and that he'll take care of me.

My days at school have also been good. I'm loved by some and envied by many; girls that is. All the girls that had been tryna get next to Jamel all year now look at me in awe. They're like, how can he want her, she's nothin' but a tenth grader. But like I said before, they don't have anything on me.

Leah and Chris are also a couple and they double date with us a lot. Most girls neglect their friends when they get a new guy in their life, but not me. Leah is the one who put me on and I'll love her forever.

Teenage Bluez

* * *

Seven Months Later

I'm getting myself ready for a date with Jamel. He's taking me to this restaurant called Uno's in that new shopping center at the Boulevard in Largo. I hear it's a tight spot. My mother had considered taking me there once. Lately, my mom and I have gotten amazingly close. We hang out at the mall shopping and getting our nails and hair done together. I knew that she would come around at the time I needed her most. She seems like she really wants to be there for me and to make sure I don't slip up and I'm willing to give her that chance.

Here I am once again primping in the mirror. This seemed so familiar because, just a few months ago, I was in this very spot stressing over what to wear so Jamel would notice me. Now I don't have to do that, he notices everything about me.

While I was putting the pins in my hair to hold my ponytail in place, I heard my cell phone ring. It was Jamel's ring tone, which was, *'My Boo,'* the song by Usher and Alicia Keys.

"Hey, boo," I said, answering my phone.

"What's up sexy? Are you ready?" he asked.

"Just about. I'm finishing up my hair. Why, what's up?"

"Nothing. I'm in the car on my way over there, but I wanted to tell you that there's been a sudden change of plans."

"Like what?" I asked curiously.

"I've changed my mind about going to Uno's. I want to do something special for you," he said mysteriously.

"Where are we going?" I asked.

"It's a surprise. You'll love it though, I'll put bread on that," he assured me.

"Okay, I'll see you when you get here."

"A'ight, sweetheart. Stay sexy and I'll see you in a few."

"Okay, boo." Then we both hung up.

As I finished doing my hair, I wondered where he could be taking me tonight. It doesn't matter, because I know that it'll be somewhere good, he always shows me a good time.

DING, DONG! I turned and looked at the clock, it was 7 o'clock on the dot. My boo was always on time. When I opened the door, Jamel was standing there with a blue bandanna in his hand and a red rose. I was used to seeing the red rose because he gave me one every time we went out, but the bandanna was something I'd never seen before.

"Hi sexy, you look real good tonight," he said, hugging me gently around the waist and planting a kiss on my forehead.

"Thank you. You look fresh yourself, baby," I said touching his chest, trying to get a feel of his pecks on the slick side.

"Okay, so where are you taking me? What's the special surprise?" I asked.

"Well, it starts with you putting this bandanna on," he said.

"Uh, I can't put that on, it doesn't even match my outfit."

"Not on your head. Over your eyes. I don't want you to see where I'm taking you."

"Oh, I get it, you're tryna be romantic. But can I trust you?" I said smiling.

"Boo, you can trust me with your life. I'm your man, ain't I?"

"Okay, put it on and then give me your arm."

"A'ight, I got you," he said, putting the bandanna over my eyes and helping me step down my porch stairs.

He held my arm until we got in his car. Sitting there blindfolded, I felt like this adventure was either going to turn out to be a total disaster or it was going to turn out good. I was hoping that it turned out good. When I asked Jamel why he wasn't talking, he said that he didn't want to slip up and mess up the surprise. But he soothed the moment by holding my hand, which made me feel much better.

After about twenty minutes, we reached our destination. I was glad because I was more than anxious to see where this special location was.

"Aerin, hold on for a minute. I want to set things up," Jamel said, getting out the car.

"A'ight, do your thing. I'll be right here," I said sarcastically.

I heard Jamel open the trunk and after about 15 minutes, he opened the car to let me out. He took my arm and led me about five feet across the grass.

"A'ight, Aerin, are you ready?" he asked standing behind me, preparing to remove the scarf.

"I'm more than ready. I thought you had left me sitting there blindfolded," I answered.

"Boo, you know I'd never do that." He took the blindfold off and stepped back.

When I looked around I was totally speechless. Our location was at a park called Lover's Lane. This is where all couples came when they wanted to have a special date. I was impressed at how he had everything laid out. It was a picnic under the stars. This wasn't normal for a 10th grader. I felt so grown up.

On the ground he had laid a blanket covered in rose petals alongside a tree with a sign that read, "Jamel and Aerin Forever," accompanied by little red hearts around our names. He also had little candles lit in different areas of the grass. Everything was so beautiful. I knew my boo had flare, but I didn't know he had this much.

"So, do you like it?" he asked, smiling from ear to ear.

"Boo, I love it," I said, hugging him. "You really outdid yourself."

As Jamel opened the picnic basket, I examined his anatomy. I found that we were dressed similar tonight; we both had on black shirts and blue jeans. His tank top complimented his perfectly cut body.

He had made B.L.T. club sandwiches, a fruit platter, chocolate covered strawberries, and he even had apple cider chilling on ice in a bucket. Talk about wining and dining a girl. If I didn't already know his age, I would've thought that he was about twenty-three.

We sat, ate and talked about life and our relationship. I fed him strawberries and he fed me cantaloupe and grapes. After we finished putting the food away, Jamel leaned his back up against the tree and I sat between his legs and rested my head comfortably on his chest. We looked out on the lake as the moon reflected upon it. That was the most beautiful sight I'd ever seen.

"Boo, I just want to say thank you for everything that you did tonight," I said.

"You're welcome, sweetheart. Aerin, I really care about you and there's nothing I wouldn't do for you. The past seven months have been an experience I won't ever forget. Who would've thought that a 17-year old guy would have his heart stolen by a 15-year old girl?" I looked up at him, unsure of where he was going. "What I'm saying is I love you, Aerin. You're everything that I look for in a female. You're smart, intelligent, sweet, and you're fine as I don't know what." He turned me around so that he could look into my eyes.

I never thought I would hear those three words come from Jamel, at least not this soon, and he sounded so sincere. It made me feel he loved me for all the right reasons that a guy is supposed to love a girl.

"Jamel, I think I love you too," I said, looking up at him.

At that moment, we shared the most passionate kiss that I've ever experienced in my life with a boy, which wasn't many. I ran my fingers gently through his dreads. When it was over, I felt so secure because he had put me in a position of comfort that I've never felt before. This was truly a night that I would never forget.

For the next ten minutes, he just held me in his strong arms and we enjoyed each other's presence. At about 10 o'clock, we got up and prepared to go home. We listened to "Love Talk and Slow Jams" on WPGC 95.5, with Todd B. and Justine Love, the whole way home. I sat back and thought about how sweet it was to be young and in love.

When we pulled up to my house, I saw the lights on in my mother's bedroom. Jamel walked me to my door, holding my hand. I thanked him again for all he did tonight. He sealed it with a kiss before he left.

When I usually got home from a date, I'd call Leah, but not tonight. I was just too consumed with how I was feeling right now. I undressed in my room and laid in bed thinking about everything that had happened tonight. I never heard my dad tell me he loves me, so to hear Jamel say he loves me was almost too good to be true. I was speechless because words couldn't express how he made me feel. I went to sleep and had wonderful dreams that night.

* * *

It had been two weeks since Jamel and I had our wonderful night. After thinking that night was the best thing that could ever happen to me, Jamel surprised me again. We were sitting on my steps one Friday night when he asked me to go with him to the prom. He was so hyped about the prom and his upcoming graduation. He told me that he was determined to do it up big. My going with him was gonna be hot because I was going to a prom before I even became a senior.

I started thinking back to a conversation I had with Leah

weeks ago about the prom.

"You know what usually happens for seniors after the prom," Leah said, nudging me.

"Yeah, yeah, yeah. All the virgins usually have sex for the first time," I said, knowing where this conversation was leading.

"Okay. Well, I have a question. Knowing where you and Jamel stand, what if he decides to take you to the prom and then he wants some as a graduation gift. Would you be willing to have sex with him?" she asked.

"Jamel knows how I feel and that I'm not ready to have sex with him. He respects that and I know he won't try and pressure me into doing anything that I don't want to do."

"Okay, that's fine. But worst-case scenario, what if you do want to do it? Temptation can get high and you can get yourself caught up in something that you'll regret later," she said seriously.

"Don't you think I know that, and that's why I'm not gonna put myself in a situation that I know I won't be able to get out of. But what about you, what if Chris wants to get busy after the prom? Will you be giving into temptation?" I said, just as serious as she was.

"Come on, Aerin, you know I ain't givin' up nothin' until I'm ready. And believe me, with Chris, I'm nowhere near ready to get busy with him," Leah said laughing.

I spent the rest of that night thinking about how I had to pick out the perfect dress and shoes, and get my hair, nails and feet done. But my real dilemma was that my mom didn't know I was dating Jamel and with the prom three weeks away, I figured since she's now tryna be a real mom it's about time she met him. I had kept him a secret from her for seven months. Before going to sleep I told myself I'd talk to her tomorrow.

When I came in the house on Saturday afternoon, I heard her in the kitchen cooking and decided to go in there and tell her about Jamel and the prom. Whatever she was cooking smelled so good.

"Hey, Ma, what you cooking?" I asked creating small talk, not wanting to jump right in.

"Spaghetti. What's up with you?" she asked, stirring a pot.

"Oh, nothing." I walked back and forth, which made me appear uneasy.

"Aerin, is something wrong?" she asked turning around, obviously bothered by my pacing.

"No, it's just that I have something to ask you, that's all," I said.

"Like what?" she asked inquisitively.

"Well, my school's senior prom is next week and I was asked to go."

"By who?" She raised her eyebrows.

"My boyfriend, Jamel, asked me." I just let it all flow out.

"Your what? He's in the 12th grade?" she asked, somewhat surprised.

"Yes, Ma'am."

"Well, how long have you and this Jamel guy been going out?" Michelle pulled a chair from the table and sat down.

She motioned for me to sit down too. I told her absolutely everything. She let me know that she wasn't happy about me keeping Jamel a secret for this long, and that she wanted to talk to him before the prom. I was so excited that she agreed to let me go on the prom, that I hugged her tightly. She said that we'd go out Wednesday night and look for my dress and accessories. I immediately called Leah to let her know how well everything went. She said that she would go with us dress hunting, which was totally fine with me.

* * *

Teenage Bluez

Prom Night

"Oh my goodness, you look gorgeous," were the words that came from my mother's lips as I opened my bedroom door. Dressed and ready for the prom, I felt like a queen. She was on the steps holding the digital camera taking my picture.

I had picked out the perfect dress. It was a beautiful Anne Klein turquoise dress that fit my form perfectly. It was adorned in diamonds around the neck. My mom had picked out the most beautiful pair of matching diamond teardrop earrings. My hair was in a beautiful pinup with spiral curls that came down in my face, and I even had diamond hairpins sparkling in my hair. I really outdid myself, of course, with the help of Leah and my mom.

I think I posed for the camera twenty times before hearing the doorbell ring. It's a good thing I'm a very photogenic person because, if I weren't she wouldn't have gotten so much footage. From the peephole view, Leah looked great.

"Ahh!" we both screamed, when I opened the door. We admired each other's look.

Leah was dressed in a cute Gucci black dress with diamonds that lined her waist and back, which was bare. Her hair was straight down to her shoulders with brown streaks. I had never seen hair so straight in my life. We were both rocking open toed stilettos from Nordstrom.

"Oh my, Leah, I need to get your picture too," my mom said, gesturing for us to get together.

While we were in the living room taking pictures, we heard a loud car horn blowing. Leah and I ran to the door and, low and behold, it was Jamel and Chris with their heads hanging out the top of a black stretch Cadillac Escalade limo sitting on 20-inch rims. Leah and I grew ecstatic. When the limo stopped, they hopped out with our corsages in hand. They were both dressed alike in black tuxedoes, hats and pimp canes.

"Hey, gorgeous," Jamel said, hugging me. "You look hot!" He held my hand, twirling me around and admiring my outfit.

"You look good too boo." I admired the fresh shape up he had which complimented his dreads that had been re-twisted and oiled. His goatee was also shaped to the bone. Leah and Chris greeted each other with a kiss.

My mom walked up behind me. Jamel, not realizing that this was my mom, simply said, "How you doing?" Then turned to me and said, "Aerin, where's your mom? I know she wants to meet me."

"Jamel, this is my mom, Ms. Michelle Washington. Mom, this is Jamel," I said, pointing to the both of them.

Jamel's whole facial expression changed. He went on to say, "Well, now I know where Aerin gets her looks from. It's good to finally meet you, and I'm indeed sorry for what just happened, Ms. Washington."

"That's alright honey, and thanks for the compliment. You're handsome yourself, and that's another thing Aerin gets from me, she knows how to pick 'em." I relaxed and smiled. "Now get going before you all are late."

"Mom, don't forget that I'm staying at Leah's tonight. I'll be home sometime tomorrow afternoon."

"Okay. You all have fun," she said, standing at the door.

We hurried down the steps and into the limo. The inside was nice; leather seats, a bottle of the bubbly and miniature TV monitors. We were definitely riding in a ride that was officially pimped out. Jamel's dad had paid for everything. Money talks when your parents have their own businesses.

We pulled up to the Embassy Suites Hotel in Crystal City, Virginia. The hotel was off the chain. It seemed as if we weren't the only ones riding in style. People were rolling up in all kinds of nice whips, everything from Mercedes, Jaguars, Hummers, to a variety of limos. A couple even rolled up on a horse drawn carriage.

Chris and Jamel jumped out of the limo first and then escorted us to the entrance of the hotel. Everybody that came looked so fly and happy. I was so ready to go inside and get my groove on. I turned and looked at Leah and we smiled at each other as if to say we made it and then we walked through the doors.

* * *

It was 12:30 am and the prom was just about over. The DJ was preparing to play the last song of the night, the jam by Alicia Keys, *'Fallin''*. Jamel pulled me onto the dance floor. While we were dancing, he whispered in my ear that he was glad I came with him tonight and he couldn't have shared this moment with anyone better. I wrapped my arms around his neck and he gripped my waist. I gave him a little peck on his lips.

As we were dancing, it seemed as if we were floating in mid-air, that's how much of a trance we were in. The song ended, the lights came on and our principal made a few last minute remarks and then went on to congratulate the seniors, wishing them luck in every endeavor. When she was done everybody started leaving. I really wasn't ready to go home. Leah and Chris looked exhausted, and why wouldn't they be, as hard as they were dancing. Jamel then made his grand announcement.

"My dad booked a suite for me tonight. Why don't we all go up there and chill for a while? We don't have to stay, but we can just kick back before going home." I secretly hoped that Chris and Leah wouldn't want to go. All night he had thought about nothing else than being alone with me.

I thought about saying no, but I wasn't quite ready to leave

Jamel and have the evening end. I figured we could hang out, maybe watch a movie and then go home. I said that it was fine with me, but Leah and Chris said they were tired and would rather go home.

I pulled Leah aside and said, "Come on, girl, stay for a little while. I'm not ready to go home right now."

"Aerin, I'm tired and sick of Chris' behind. I really don't want to spend any more time with him. I think you should come back to my place too. But if you're sure you want to go with Jamel, you know I'll cover for you. You're my girl. Just remember, don't do anything just because he wants you to."

"Jamel's not like that," I said, in his defense.

"Whatever, Aerin. I'll see you when you get to my house. And don't be bringing your butt in too late, waking me up to let you in."

"Okay. And Leah, thanks for having my back."

After we said our goodbyes, Jamel wrapped his arm around me and led me to an elevator to a fifth floor suite. I asked him how was I supposed to get back to Leah's house when they took the limo. He assured me that he had parked his Cadillac here earlier and that he'd drop me off in a couple of hours.

When the elevator doors opened, we walked down the hall to Room 505. He stuck the key in and when he opened the door, the room looked like a mini apartment. It had an area that had a couch, love seat, Playstation II, a TV with cable, and a fully stocked mini bar. In the back was the bedroom, which had a huge king size bed with a crisp white comforter and a TV with cable also. The bed was scattered with rose petals. In the bathroom there was a huge Jacuzzi/tub with a shower off to the side.

"Jamel, this is really nice," I said, not believing that I was really in a hotel suite with a guy. I knew right then that I should turn around and leave before I did something I was going to live to regret.

"That's why I picked it, it's the best suite on this floor," he said, happy that I was impressed.

I pulled off my heels, got the remote and flopped down on the bed. The bed was so comfortable and the fabric felt good on my skin. Jamel told me that he had to use the bathroom. I just sat there flipping through the channels. I finally found an episode of Martin. I just loved Martin and Gina's relationship. I hoped one day Jamel and I could be like them. When Jamel came out of the bathroom, he just had his wifebeater and boxers on.

"Jamel, I thought we were coming up here to just chill for a while?" I asked, getting nervous.

"Yo, It' hot. I just wanted to cool off from all that dancing tonight. Aren't you hot?" He hopped on the bed beside me. "Um, boo, you smell good." He kissed my neck.

"A lady is supposed to always smell good," I said, still nervous.

"I know that's right," he said, rubbing my leg.

Martin came back on and we sat watching the half hour show, laughing the whole time. When the show was over, I turned and laid my head on Jamel's chest.

"Hey, boo, do you think we could ever be like Martin and Gina?" he asked.

"That's the same thing that I was just thinking. If we stay strong, then we can be," I answered.

"Alright, as long as you don't play me, I'm cool." He stroked my hair gently.

"I won't ever play you, trust me. I want you to know that I'm so proud of you. Here you are about to graduate and go to college. Are you ready for the real world?"

"You sound just like my mom and dad. Yeah, I'm ready, but thanks for your concern for me." He kissed me softly on the cheek. "Do you want to know what I'm proud of?" he asked.

"What?" I asked smiling.

"I'm proud to say that you're my girl and that I love you."

"I love you too, boo." I gave him a peck on the mouth.

That peck led to us looking deep into each other's eyes, and that deep look led to a deeper kiss. The kiss was just like the one we shared at Lover's Lane, but only sweeter. I don't know what happened, but the next thing I knew, Jamel was on top of me. I was so caught up in the moment that I didn't even pay that any attention. But reality began to set in when he started taking off my dress. When I realized that I was down to my bra and panties, I pushed him off of me. I caught him off guard.

"I can't do this." I said, sitting up.

"Boo, what's wrong? I thought you loved me?"

"I do love you, it's just that I'm scared," I said. "I'm not ready for sex?"

"Why would I make you feel scared or hurt you for that matter? I thought you trusted me."

"I do trust you, but things are just happening too fast."

"I'm sorry, but I'm really hurt right now. Why don't you trust me?" he said, almost yelling. I saw the frustration in his eyes.

"I do trust you, Jamel. I'm just nervous." I had never seen Jamel so mad before. I couldn't hold back the tears.

"Oh no, Aerin, don't cry. I'm sorry that I made you feel scared. I didn't mean to rush you. I'm sorry for getting upset. Come on, stop crying." He pulled me into his arms and consoled me.

His touch felt so good to me at that moment. I don't know what came over me, but the next thing I knew, I was all over him tears and all. Jamel asked me if I was sure I wanted to do this, and I said, "Yes". I felt so much passion between us. When we made love, I actually felt the love that we had for each other. He was gentle with me and I felt like a woman. When it was over, he just held me in his arms and told me that he loved me. I made him promise to hold me until I said for him to let me go.

*   *   *

Oh, my God, was all I could say to myself when I woke up and looked at the clock. When I saw that the clock read 7:00 the next morning, I jumped out of the bed so fast you would have thought someone poured cold water on me. I went to the other side of the bed and shook Jamel.

"Jamel, it's 7:00 in the morning, you have to get me home! My mom is gonna kill me." I panicked.

"Man, I didn't mean to fall asleep," he said, getting up and rushing to get his clothes on.

I'm pretty sure by now my mom knows I didn't stay at Leah's because I know her mom, without a doubt, got worried and called my mom.

Jamel and I were checked out of the hotel by 7:15. On the way home, I was so focused on getting there that I almost forgot about everything that had happened earlier. I don't know how it could've slipped my mind, because that was the reason why I was in this mess. But I guess right now, I was thinking more about having to face my mom. I did acknowledge the fact that I could no longer call myself a virgin. It was almost hard to believe. I would've never thought I would be only fifteen and having sex. I sat quietly the entire ride home, which was about a thirty-minute drive.

When we pulled up to my house, I said goodbye to Jamel and got ready to get out of the car. He grabbed my arm before I could get out.

"What's wrong?" he asked.

"Nothing, I'm alright. Why?"

"I don't know, it just seems as if you're a little upset." He rubbed my shoulder.

"No, I'm not mad. I'm just thinking about what happened last night," I said. "And the fact that my mom is gonna kill me."

"Well, are you tryna say that you regret what we did?" he asked, sounding offended.

"No, it's not like that. It's just that I can no longer say that I'm a virgin. Since this isn't your first time having sex, you're not moved by all of this. This is something huge to me." I tried to get him to understand where I was coming from.

I loved Jamel and I knew he loved me, but I didn't know if I had made a mistake by giving myself to him. Jamel said that he'd give me a chance to regroup. I kissed him on the cheek and told him that I'd call him later depending on how my mom reacted once I got in the house.

When I got out of the car, I had such a lump in my throat that it became hard to swallow. I was so nervous because I didn't know what I was going to say to her to keep her from killing me. When I got to the front door, I just stood there for a minute and took a deep breath. There was no point in me losing it because I would have to face her whether I panicked or not, so I decided to get it together.

I put my key in the door, turned the knob and opened the door slowly. When I got inside, she wasn't in the living room or the kitchen. I thought maybe she was either still asleep or not home. But when I heard the music in the back room I started to get nervous again. I closed the door lightly and walked to the back towards my room, but she met me on the way to my room. *Shoot!*

"Mom," I said, startled.

"Don't mom me. Where have you been?" she asked, clearly upset. "Hello? Now you can't say anything? Leah's mom called and told me that you didn't come to her house last night. Now where have you been?" she asked again, this time very firmly.

I was hesitant to speak. "I was at the hotel with Jamel," I said.

"You were what? Why did you stay with that boy? You should've brought yourself back to Leah's!" she said, yelling at me.

I started walking to my room and she followed me. "Mom, I only stayed because he said that his Dad had booked the suite. Why pay for something and not use it," I said.

"Why were you the only one to stay? Leah seemed to be able to bring her behind home!"

"Yeah. She and Chris were tired and they decided to go home."

"So you stayed with Jamel? Did you have sex with that boy?" she asked.

I didn't answer her. What was I supposed to say?

"Hello, there's that dead silence again. I asked you whether you had sex with him?" she shouted.

The first thing that came out of my mouth was, "No, Mom, I didn't have sex with Jamel." She knew I was lying. I then got up to go to my closet and change my clothes.

"Aerin, don't lie to me! Did you have sex with Jamel?" I didn't say anything. "I knew it! I knew you were out there slummin' around with those boys, and it was only a matter of time before you screwed up! I try my best to be there for you and you do something like this. You're going to be a big disappointment just like your dad," she said, in a harsh tone.

I just stood there wishing she'd leave, but she continued with her speech. "You young girls think y'all grown enough to be out here havin' sex. That is until the boy doesn't want you anymore or when you end up pregnant. And then when he dumps you, who do you run home to, Mommy! Aerin, I'm tellin' you now, if you wanna be grown and have sex with Jamel, then you betta be prepared to suffer any consequences that may occur."

I couldn't believe what I was hearing. I turned and looked at her as if she was crazy.

"Mom, who are you to talk about anyone being a disappointment? You just started paying me any attention! You missed out on nearly five years of my life because you spent them catering to yourself, your job and your boyfriends! Just because you come to me now tryna play the good Mommy role no one is going to applaud you," I said.

"Don't you ever use that tone with me! You want to live your life being a whore, then go right ahead, but don't try and make me feel like it's my fault! You know that you could've cared less whether I was here or not!" She was yelling at the top of her lungs.

I backed away from her. With every word that came out of her mouth, I knew that the past few months that we had spent together had been nothing less than phony.

"Well, you know what Mom, I did have sex with Jamel! He was my first and I'm not going to live my life as a whore! I'm not like you!" I screamed.

She hauled off and slapped me in the face. "Get the heck out of my house! I told you not to use that tone with me," she said.

"I swear if you weren't my mom I would kill you! But two wrongs don't make a right. You only treat me this way because you were treated this way, and I'd rather you put me out then for you to ever put your hands on me again." I walked away. I got everything I needed and was on my way.

On my way out of the door, she called my name and said, "Aerin, just know that you'll never be anything in life without me! You're going to be back!"

"I doubt it. The only time I'll be back is to get the rest of my stuff." I closed the door behind me.

It took everything in my power to keep from falling apart.

But I couldn't hold back the tears because I was so hurt. To hear someone say those things broke my heart, but for my mom to be that someone killed me. I never thought something like this would happen between my mom and me. Especially considering how close we had become over the last few months. All I did was have sex, and that has cost me my mom and a place to lay my head. Jamel was the first guy I had been with, but was it going to continue? No, because I refused to live up to any of the names my mom labeled me with. I just didn't know what to do about a place to live.

As I was walking down the street, I started to think about where I was going to go. When I came up on Crown Street, the answer came to me. Leah's house was on the right hand side. I felt like I had no other choice, she was the only person I had now. When I knocked on the door, I realized that it was only 9:30 in the morning and I was probably waking them up. Jus came and answered the door. She looked like she had been up for a while because she was already dressed.

"Oh my God, Aerin, what's wrong?" she said, when she opened the door. She pulled me inside. "Leah, I think you should come out here!" she yelled to her sister.

"What?" Leah said, not noticing me at first. "Oh my God, Aerin, what happened to your eye and why are you crying?" she asked. I hadn't even known that I had a mark on my face.

I told them everything that happened with me and Jamel and the situation with my mom. Leah told me that she was gonna let her mom know what happened and ask her if I could stay with them for a while. She was sure that her mom wouldn't mind me staying there. After that, we sat up and talked. I couldn't stop crying, and Leah consoled me until I eventually fell asleep.

* * *

"Oh no, this can't be!" I said to Leah, as she read aloud the pregnancy book that Jus had gotten from the local library.

Everything the book said were signs of pregnancy, the same signs I had been experiencing. It had been more than a month since Jamel and I had sex. For the last three weeks I had been throwing up and I had missed my period. The book also said something about heavy eating and going to the bathroom a lot. I've been peeing like a Kentucky Derby racehorse, eating Leah's family out of house and home, and I've been sleeping like a bear during the winter when it's hibernating. All of this matched up with the book, but I still wasn't convinced that I was pregnant.

I told Leah that we had to go to the corner store and buy a pregnancy test. I didn't know what I was going to do if I was pregnant. I'm only fifteen, what can I do for a child? I hadn't talked to Jamel in two days. So I decided to give him a call. He really wants to go to Florida State University, and I believe he can go. He can get into any college that he wants with his grades. He knows about everything that happened between my mom and me. He offered to let me stay with him, but I told him that's what got me in the situation that I was in now.

Jamel's phone rang twice before he answered. "Hello."

"Hey boo. How are you?" I asked.

"I'm okay," he said, sounding a bit down.

"What's wrong?"

"Nothing. I'm just a little depressed because no school has responded to my applications yet."

"Somebody will respond soon. I don't see why they wouldn't," I said, trying to be supportive.

"Thanks boo, I hope so."

We talked for about an hour then he said that he loved me and that he hoped to see me this weekend. My thoughts quickly skipped back to this pregnancy thing. If I am, how do I tell

Jamel that he's going to be a father? How will he react? Leah came in the room and told me that she was ready to go to the store. I got my jacket and then we headed out.

*   *   *

"Aerin, what does it say?" Leah yelled from outside the bathroom door.

"Wait, I didn't even pee on it yet!"

"Just remember that a plus sign means positive, and a minus means negative," Jus said.

"Okay," I said, as I got myself prepared. My heart was beating so fast that I was shaking. I almost couldn't get my urine out. When I finally did, I remembered the directions said that it would take thirty seconds to reveal whether or not you're pregnant. I waited thirty seconds and then I looked at my test. I felt like I was having a heart attack.

"What does it say, Aerin?" Leah and Jus said.

I couldn't speak. I opened the door and the tears began to fall from my face.

"Well, what is it?" Leah asked.

The words came out slowly, but surely. "Pregnant," I said, in a shaky voice.

"Oh, Aerin, it's going to be okay," Jus said, as she and Leah came to comfort me.

I couldn't help myself, I cried and cried. Leah and Jus were really supportive. They asked me if I wanted to tell their mom. I told them not until I figured out what I was going to do. They stayed up with me for as long as they could, but then I told them that I would be all right and that I needed some alone time to think this through.

I couldn't be mad because all of this was a consequence of me making a bad decision. I now had to think about taking on the responsibility of being a teenage mother, and that was something I vowed I would never be. I was so confused because there were people that had sex all the time and had no children, but the first time I have sex I get pregnant. What can I offer a child and I'm just a child myself? Everything happened before I even had a chance to think about my life, what I wanted to do, what I wanted to be, and whom I wanted to be with. I definitely didn't want to be a mother right now, but I didn't do this by myself. How was I gonna tell Jamel that I'm carrying his kid? I didn't know what his reaction would be. Jamel loves me and I knew this was going to be a huge shock to him, but he's a pretty responsible guy. I knew if I didn't have support from anyone, that he would support me. It was only about 11 o'clock at night, so I figured he might still be up.

"Hello," he said, sounding as if he was asleep. I got tense instantly.

"Jamel, what you doin?" I asked.

"Hey, boo. I'm not doing anything right now. Why?"

"I have something to tell you. I…." he cut me off.

"Wait, before you do that, do you think I can come scoop you up tomorrow? We have something to celebrate," he said.

"Yeah, sure," I said. That would be better because this was something he should be told face to face.

"So, what do you have to tell me?" he asked.

"Oh, I guess it can wait until tomorrow."

"Alright, boo. I'm goin' to sleep but I can't wait to see you tomorrow. Love you," he said.

"I love you too, Jamel." Then we both hung up.

After hanging up, I sat and thought about how was I gonna tell Jamel that I was pregnant. I thought about it all night.

I woke up the next morning throwing up just like I did every other morning. I guess this is something that I was gonna have to get used to. Jamel called and said that he'd be here at noon.

He also said that I was really going to be proud of him.

* * *

"Aerin, are you okay?" Leah asked, as I was getting dressed.
"I guess so, Leah. This is just something I have to deal with."
"You'll be alright. Just know that I'm here for you."
"Thanks, Leah," I said, hugging her.
I heard Jamel's horn at noon on the dot. I said goodbye to Leah and went out the door. Usually when Jamel comes to get me I have the biggest smile on my face, but not today. It was because I knew what I knew about myself and he didn't. I opened the car door and got in. He gave me a kiss.
"Hey boo, I missed you," he said, as we drove off.
"I missed you too. So, where are we going today?"
"Oh, somewhere that's real familiar, just sit tight. I'll tell you the good news when we get there." He smiled.
Jamel talked about nothing in general the whole time it took to get to our destination. I really wasn't listening, my mind was focused on what I was about to tell him and how he was gonna take it. When I saw where we were I was surprised. He had taken me back to Lover's Lane. *This must really be something special that he wants to celebrate*, I thought.
He took me to the exact spot that he had taken me to before, and it was even more beautiful during the day. He told me that he wanted us to just sit here and chill for a while. Then he was going to take me to the Olive Garden. He sat down at the same tree, grabbed my hand and pulled me down to him.
"Jamel, what is it that you have to tell me?" I asked.
"Okay, I'ma tell you. But when I finish, I want you to say what you were gonna tell me the other night."
"Okay, now tell me your news," I said, unable to wait any

longer to hear what he had to say.

"Remember when I told you about no one responding to my applications?" I shook my head yes. "Well, I've been accepted to Florida State and Howard University. I chose Florida State and they want me to start in September." He was really excited.

"Boo, that's so great!" I hugged him tightly.

"Thanks. I'm just so happy right now. So what is it that you have to tell me?" That changed the whole mood when he said that. I didn't know where to start.

"Okay. Jamel, this is kind of hard for me, so just bare with me." I couldn't hold back the tears. That's another thing with pregnancy, you're an emotional wreck. "Do you remember the night of your prom when we shared ourselves with one another? Well, that night made us have to share something else also," I said, crying even harder.

"Aerin, what is it? Why are you crying?"

"Jamel, I'm pregnant! You're gonna be a daddy!"

"I'm gonna be a what? You have to be kiddin' me!" He let go of my hand and stood up. "I can't be a father!"

"You're the only one that I've been with so, without a doubt, you're the father." I couldn't believe that he was acting this way.

"So, what are you going to do about it?" he asked.

"Well, I was thinking that maybe I could come stay with you and we would be in this together."

"No way, I can't do a baby right now! I'm about to go off to college in two months. I have plans for my life. This is too much for me! We can't keep this kid!" He shook his head and walked towards the car. I got up and followed him.

"So, are you implying that I get an abortion? Because if you are, there's no way that I'm doing that! I don't have the right to take anyone's life away, especially an innocent baby!" By now we were standing outside of his car.

"Well, you have no other choice! You're only fifteen and I'm seventeen, and what do we have? Nothing! I just can't understand how you got pregnant anyway."

"Well, like they say it takes two to tango." I thought back to that night and suddenly I didn't remember Jamel wearing a condom because everything had happened so fast. "Jamel, did you have on a condom when we had sex?" I asked him.

He hesitated. "Well, no," he finally said.

"How could you not put on a condom?"

"Because I wasn't prepared to have sex that night."

"Okay, but now you have to be responsible for what you did. We both have to be responsible."

"Boo, you know I love you but you have to abort this baby. This is too much for the both of us and you know that," he said, pleadingly.

"Of course I know that, that's why I'm so indecisive. But if I kill my baby, I'll never be able to forgive myself."

"That's something we'll both have to deal with. But you're young and you have plenty of time to have kids when you're older. Just think about it," he begged.

I had nothing to say. I just got in the car and cried. Jamel got in and I told him to take me back to Leah's. I hated him at that moment. It's like he turned into a totally different person. How could he say that he loved me and then tell me to take our child's life? I just didn't understand that. But there was still a part of me that saw where he was coming from. We don't have anything to give a baby. I also knew that I couldn't give it up for adoption because if I couldn't have my child I didn't want anybody else to have it. I really had to do some serious thinking. When we pulled up to Leah's, Jamel stopped me from getting out of the car.

"What Jamel?" I said.

"I know that you're mad, but here's three hundred dollars if you decide to get rid of the baby. If you don't, then I'm afraid that we can't be together. I'll always love you, I just can't have a baby with you," he said, handing me the money.

I took the money, got out of his car, and he drove off. I went in the house hurt and betrayed. I felt like I had no one. Now I see know how the girls on the Maury show feel. I used to crack on them, but now I was almost in the same position. The only difference was I knew who my baby daddy was. I guess what you knock is what you become.

I went into Leah's room and sat on the end of her bed. She came in and asked me how everything went with Jamel.

"Well, he gave me three hundred dollars for an abortion," I said sadly.

"So, what are you going to do? You're not going to do it, are you?" Leah asked.

"I don't know, Leah. I don't want to do it, but what other choice do I have?"

"There is assistance out here, you don't have to kill your baby. Jamel is a real jerk for even suggesting that."

"Well, what can he do? He's going to college, he can't help me," I said. "It's my fault for being stupid. I should've kept my legs closed."

"He helped you get it, so what he can do is be a man and take care of his responsibility. He's taking the easy way out by tellin' you to get rid of it," she said. "Maybe we should tell my mom or yours."

"No, please don't say anything to your mom. And as far as my mom goes, when she slapped and threw me out the house that was the end of our relationship. She told me that I was gonna need her and I'll be darn if I prove her right," I said. Even though right now I wanted nothing more than to have my mother take me in her arms and tell me that everything was gonna be alright, I knew that wasn't possible. I was gonna have to handle this alone.

"Leah, I need you by my side. I don't have anybody but you. Will you go with me to get an abortion?" I pleaded with her.

"Okay, Aerin. When do you want to go?" she said, giving in to me.

"I'ma call and make an appointment for Saturday."

I had made my decision. It wasn't a decision that I wanted to make, but I had to save myself heartache. I just pray that the Lord will forgive me for my decision.

*   *   *

"Take this to the waiting room and fill it out in its entirety. When you're finished bring it back and place it in this box, sweetheart," the nurse said to me, as she gave me some paperwork to fill out.

I was at St. Joseph's Medical Center with Leah by my side. I went over to the waiting area to complete the paperwork. At first I thought I would be the only person there, but about seven other girls were in the room. Some came with their mom, others with friends, and some came alone. As I was sitting there, it crossed my mind that eight little babies would never get a chance at life.

Being as though I was only fifteen, I had to lie about my age because, if not, they would have wanted my mother's consent. When I finished the paperwork, I took it to the front desk where the nurse was and placed it in the box. When I came back, Leah sat there mute. She had already said that she was only there to support me. I told her that I had to go to the bathroom and asked if she wanted to come with me. She said no because they might call my name while we were gone.

On the way to the bathroom, I read the many posters that they had plastered all over the place. It seemed like every one of them said something to me. There was one that talked about how a baby is aborted every thirty minutes. One that talked about how every time you abort a baby that's one less person that could have made a difference in the world, and the last one was a picture of a little boy that grew up to be a medical doctor. But it wouldn't have happened if his mom had taken his life away. On my way back from the bathroom, I wondered whether I was doing the right thing. Would I be able to live with the guilt? But I felt like it was too late because I was already there.

When I got back to the waiting room, Leah was sitting with her hands over her face. For a minute I thought she was crying, but then she removed her hands. As we sat and waited, we heard screams from the back room that frightened me. When I heard the screams again, that's when I started to get nervous. I got up and went to the front desk to speak with the nurse.

"Excuse me, but I'm curious. During the procedure, are we put to sleep or do we remain awake?" I asked the nurse.

"Honey, you're awake. You're given local anesthesia," she said.

"Okay, thanks." I turned and walked away.

Just when I thought I wasn't nervous enough, she goes and tells me something like that. It's bad enough that I'm taking part in my child's death, but I have to see my child being sucked out of my body. I had a whole heap of thoughts running through my mind. Right at that moment, a female who looked to be around my age came from the back area in a wheelchair crying. She was being pushed by a woman I assumed was her mother. All she kept saying as her mother tried to comfort her was that she couldn't believe that she did it.

Leah turned to me crying and said, "Aerin, do you see that? If you go through with this you're crazy." She then got up and told me she would be in the car.

All I could do was cry because this wasn't something that I wanted to do.

"Aerin Lewis, we're ready for you," I heard the nurse say. I got up and walked to the front desk.

* * *

Ten years later

"Ma, the phone. It's Aunty Leah!" Troy yelled, from the kitchen.

"Okay, I have it. What's up, Lee?" I said.

"Girl, nothing. I'm calling because I wanted to see what you were gonna do for Troy's birthday."

"I think I'm going to take him out. He's ten now so he's too big for Chucky Cheese," I said.

"Alright, that's fine. Just let me know."

"Okay, bye." We both hung up.

Here I am twenty-five years old and happy. I graduated from high school on time, went to college, and I didn't have to abort my son to do it. It wasn't easy, but every time I look at my son I'm glad I didn't abort him. Leah, Jus and their mom were by my side through it all.

I'm not gonna say that it was easy, because it wasn't. Once I made the decision to keep my child, I no longer got to hang out at the mall, I missed my senior prom, and I had to grow up very quickly. After Troy was born, I was no longer invited to parties, and I didn't live the life of an average teenager. If I had to do it all over again, I would've never went with Jamel to that hotel room the night of his prom.

I'm the owner of my own Hair Shop and business is booming. I have a fiancé that supports me in everything I do and we plan on getting married next spring. He's been a good male figure in Troy's life, I couldn't ask for anyone better. I don't know where I would be if I would've stayed at that clinic.

If I hadn't realized that Troy was a gift from God, then I wouldn't be the woman I am today and I wouldn't have my testimony.

I haven't seen my mom since the day I went back to get the rest of my belongings from her house. My cousin says that she's now confined to a wheelchair. But like they say what comes around, goes around. I don't hate her, but I'm still hurt about how she threw me out and basically disowned me. I haven't heard anything from my dad, which is no surprise.

Jamel, I hear owns a successful car dealership and he's going to school for his Masters. After he gave me that money to kill our son, I never saw him again. He doesn't even know if his child is dead or alive. But it doesn't matter because I've been a mother and father to our son.

Leah got married to Chris five years ago, and they have a little girl who is three years old, named Mya. Who would have thought that would have happened? Jus is going to law school and she's been busting straight A's.

Looking back on my life and all the changes that I've been through helps me see what I was missing in my life. I was missing the man who orchestrates everything, God. Now that I have Him, I can't go wrong.

"Ma, c'mon the movie is starting," Troy said.

Well, my child is calling for me. I have to go be a mommy.

PHAT AS I WANNA BE
by Ashley Jones

I shivered as I waited for Dr. Joyner to return to my hospital room. I didn't want to be here and he was taking forever to come back to take my temperature. The white walls were driving me crazy and the bloating I felt in my stomach would not go away.

Finally, Dr. Joyner came into the room, thermometer in hand.

"Malissa, open wide and say ahhh," he said.

"Ahhh," I responded blandly. Before I knew it, vomit started coming up. I knocked the thermometer out of my mouth and made a dash for the wastebasket.

"I'm so sorry, Dr. Joyner." He handed me some paper towels to wipe my mouth.

"It's not your fault, dear. Now do you think we can do this again, without the throw up?" he chuckled.

Before I could answer, my mother said, "That child is so dramatic."

I cut my eyes at her as Dr. Joyner stuck the thermometer into my mouth for the second time. My mother loved to describe me as a drama queen. When I had cramps, I was being dramatic. When I was in the 5th grade and broke my collarbone while playing dodge ball, I was accused of acting dramatic. When I got strep throat and had a fever of 105 degrees and could barely walk, I was accused of being dramatic. I had to literally be lying on my deathbed to get some attention from this woman.

My stomach made a loud growling noise as I got up to look at myself in the hospital mirror. All I had eaten today was a bag of UTZ potato chips. My size three body looked like a size 16 instead. Although I had just been weighed in at exactly 108 pounds, I felt so fat. Even though I was starving, I told myself that I'd have to do without dinner tonight.

"Ah choo!" I had been sneezing like crazy these past couple of weeks.

I continued the self-examination of myself in the mirror. I felt so ugly. My brown shoulder length hair looked dry and dull, and my once beautiful, dark brown eyes looked teary. The blue dingy hospital gown that I was wearing only made me feel worse. Knowing that I would be in the hospital until the next day, I crawled into the hospital bed, pulled the blankets over my head, and silently cried myself to sleep.

* * *

"Your daughter is free to go," I heard Dr. Joyner say the next morning.

"Good, cause I'm ready to get up out this dang hospital," my mom said, whippin' out her cell phone to check the time. "Pack her up and let's go. I have better things that I can be doing other than hanging around this hospital." She looked in the mirror above the bed and said, "I need to call Tracy so I can schedule an early hair appointment for tomorrow. This stuff looks like who shot John and why they did it!"

That was a typical thing for her to say even in the midst of an emergency. When we thought our house would catch fire because the one next to us did, the first thing she packed up was her make-up.

"We need to look good no matter what," I can remember her saying, as I had watched her pack other items in record speed.

Dr. Joyner said, "Well, ma'am, we really don't know what's going on with Malissa right now. We've done several tests but we still have no results." Sighing, he added, "Being with her for these past few days, I can tell you what I think is wrong, but I'd rather not assume."

Paying no attention to Dr. Joyner at all, my mom said, "Well, hey, I guess she'll be a'ight then. There probably wasn't nothin' wrong with her in the first place." She snatched the release papers from Dr. Joyner. "Just let me sign these papers and get on up outta here." I was being released from the hospital without a diagnosis.

As soon as I was wheeled out the door, I stood and looked around for mom's Mazda 626. I was surprised to see her new SL500 Mercedes Benz because I was never allowed to ride in it for fear that I'd spill something on the Louis Vutton interior.

My mother, Veronica Tucker, was what they called a red-bone out in B-more. She rocked long, dark brown hair with blonde streaks, and visited the hair salon twice a week. She was very petite and fellas often threw her compliments on her coke bottle figure and light brown eyes. Her beauty was her pride and joy.

We got in the car and proceeded to go home. I was doing fine for about fifteen minutes, then I started feeling nauseous again. My throat started burning and before I knew it, I was rolling down my mom's precious car windows to puke.

"Chile, are you spitting up in my car? Are you crazy?" she asked, while checking her make-up in the rear view mirror. "And why are you still vomiting anyway? Those doctors swore up and down you were alright. Doctors these days don't know nothin'. They sit up in medical school for however many years, take notes, then all of a sudden they're doctors. And another thing, are you pregnant?"

"No," I answered softly, clutching my stomach in pain. Boy, I'd give anything to be with my father right now.

When we finally pulled up into the driveway of our house, I got out of the car and made a mad dash to my bedroom. I put on my pink, silk Victoria's Secret pajama set that my daddy had purchased for my birthday. I dimmed the lights and stared at the walls and the dresser adorned with awards and trophies. From track to cheerleading, I had done it all. I looked at pictures of me smiling and happy. I was skinner in those days.

There was no way that I was going to the Annual Hair Show next month with my best friends, Jessica and CiCi, looking like this. We were supposed to go shopping for our outfits after school tomorrow. How could I expect to fit into anything looking so pudgy?

Ring! Ring! Ring! I definitely wasn't in the mood to talk to anyone.

"Malissa, Jessica is on the phone!" my mom yelled up to me.

Picking up the phone and biting my nails, I hollered, "I have it, Mom. You can hang up now." She had a knack for listening in on my conversations. Once we knew she hung up, Jessica said, "Hey, girl, what's up? Where have you been? We haven't seen you in school lately."

"I've been sick for a while," I said. "But I'll be in school tomorrow because I'm feeling much better."

From the bottom of the steps, my mom yelled once again. "Malissa, sweetie, you need to hurry up and get off the phone because I have a very important call to make to a client. Then when I get off you need to call your hillbilly father because he's been calling like crazy."

"Okay, Mom!" I yelled back. Returning my attention back to Jessica, I said, "Hello."

"I heard what your Mom just said, so give me a call later on.

Oh, make sure you're in school tomorrow because we need to get back to our planning for the Annual Hair Show."

"Okay, I'm sure I'll be there tomorrow. Thanks again for calling to check on me," I said, ending our conversation.

Knowing that everyone was going to ask where I had been, I laid on my bed contemplating what I would tell them. Should I say it was a common cold, a severe fever or that I just needed a little time off from school? I didn't know what I'd say since I had been away from school for almost a week. Yet, I knew that I had to think of something that wouldn't have people curious about what was really going on with me, especially Jessica and CiCi.

Jessica was too smart, she had street and book smarts. She was the shortest, fliest chick that ever walked the halls at Burnside High. She was 5'2, with a small frame, and toted a booty most males dreamed of. Her nickname at school was dunka-dunk. Everyone thought she had some type of Indian in her because her hair was naturally long, soft, and beautiful. She walked around always swinging her hair, while constantly in the halls skipping every other class. Yet she was real cool to hang out with.

CiCi wasn't your average, dark skinned chick. She rocked the short haircut similar to Halle Berry, except hers was often spiked. She was about 5'4, up to date with her style of clothes and cared less what another person had to say about her. CiCi was into doing her schoolwork and didn't really get out the house much. But was real cool to chill and hang with when she could get out.

* * *

My mom walked into my room without knocking. She walked over to my bed, took a seat and started filing down her already perfectly shaped nails. She watched me from the corner of her eye before speaking.

"Hey, Malissa, please call your father. I'm sick and tired of every time that I'm on the phone handling some business he interrupts me with his foolishness." Mimicking him with a sassy, hostile voice, she said, *"Hey, Veronica, can you please put my baby girl on the phone? I'd like to speak to her for a moment."*

Clutching my stomach, I said, "Mom, I'ma call him, but why is it that every time you tell me to call my dad you have to go on and on about what he's doing or what he has to say?" Turning my back on her, I looked in the mirror at the naval ring I had begged her for, and continued. "Oh, and another thing, you're taking this law firm thing a little too serious. You've only been working there for almost a month. Maybe you shouldn't be so worried about getting work done when you're not at the office." I walked away from the mirror to turn on the radio and sat on the bed.

"That job isn't going anywhere," I continued. "It's not going to grow feet and walk away from you in the middle of the night. If my opinion mattered, I'd say that's exactly why they hired you in the first place." Not daring to stare her in the eyes, I quickly added, "They needed someone who likes runnin' on and on about stuff that isn't even that important, and who only has at least two years at a nearby community college."

I could tell that my mother was tempted to slap me across my sassy mouth, but I didn't care. She had it coming.

"Yeah, I went to a community college for two years and got a job at a big time law firm as a receptionist! I did it so stop hatin'!" she yelled. "And I don't care about your sorry, bald headed father. He's fat and ain't worth a dime. The divorce papers are on the way to his door. And another thing, I'm the mother in this house!" My mother shook her finger a mile a minute as her cheeks turned bright red. "If you think you're gonna lay up in my house and talk to me like you're crazy and still expect for me to take care of your sickly tail, you got another thing comin'. Especially if you're pregnant, because it sure seems like that's the problem. You keep spittin' up a lot, sleeping and holdin' that dang belly of yours. Chile, don't let that be the diagnoses them doctors didn't see!" She slammed the door.

"The truth hurts, doesn't it!" I yelled to her.

I picked up the phone to call my daddy. I didn't know what I would say if he answered the phone. My mom, or should I say, Veronica, had really struck a nerve. I knew I wasn't pregnant because I've never had sex. And just maybe if she'd paid a little more attention to me, I could talk to her about this so-called sex thing.

After the fourth ring, his answering machine came on. "Hello, you've reached the voice mailbox of Matthew Tucker. I'm unable to answer your call at the moment, but leave me a detailed message and I'll give you a call back. And if this is my baby gal, Lissa calling, I love you honey." Beeeeeep.

"Wow," I whispered. I really didn't expect his answering machine to say that. My daddy and I were close, but not as close as we should be. One of the reasons is that he lived in Louisiana and we lived in Baltimore. My mom didn't make matters any better, either.

"That man is no good," she would constantly say or, "You couldn't pay me a million dollars to get back with that man!"

My daddy was handsome, but he was also overweight. He had a way of getting under mom's skin. Whenever he made her mad, she would take her revenge out on me by saying, "Ya know, you're looking more and more like that man everyday, the spittin' image of him. I swear I must be cursed." Other times when we'd go shopping at the mall, she'd say things like, "You're not as skinny as you used to be. You got that from your father's side of the family."

When she'd say things like that, I'd cry myself to sleep at night. Some days I'd go without eating. She never seemed to notice, though. In her eyes, I was just an attention seeker. I was just like my daddy. I was so lost in my own thoughts that I didn't even notice that she came back into my room.

"Hey, Malissa, what did your father say?" she asked, out of nosiness. As much as she said she couldn't stand that man, she was always asking about him. It was only so that she could continue her tirade of talking bad about him. Remembering the argument that we had earlier, encouraged me not to feed into her madness.

"Nothing much. He just wanted to see how I was doing in school and if I wanted to catch a plane out to the farm next weekend. That's about it. Why?"

"So, are you going out to the farm? He might give you some money toward that hairstyle you plan on getting for that Fashion Show. I sure can't afford it till this case I'm working on is settled," she said, trying to see what my thoughts were about seeing him.

"Yes, Mom, I'm going to go. And it's not a Fashion Show, it's a Hair Show," I said dryly.

"Well, I just knew it was some show that you've been dying to attend for the past two months. Are you and those chicks you hang out with at school going to finish looking for y'all outfits tomorrow?" she asked. She wasn't really looking for an answer to the question because she knew that she was beginning to get on my nerves again. "Honey, I'm going downstairs to finish supper. It should be ready in about thirty minutes or so. You've gotta be starving."

She was proud of herself because she had cooked for once. The only other times she cooked was when company came over. Relieved that she left out of my room and stopped buggin' me,

I went back to thinking about what I would tell CiCi and Jessica in school tomorrow. Finally, I decided that I was gonna tell them that my mom had been sick, and while taking care of her, I caught a cold from her.

I didn't feel like eating, but I felt kind of bad for the way that I had talked to my mom earlier. I decided to go downstairs to eat dinner as a truce. At the table, I forced my body to accept the pork chops smothered in gravy with a side of rice and corn. I didn't even notice my mom watching me as I threw down.

"Honey, are you okay?" she asked.

"Yes, Mom, I'm fine. I haven't eaten all day and these chops are the bomb. Why must you always ask am I alright?" I was eager to know why she would complain about me actually eating all of my food for a change.

"Sweetie, I just thought I'd ask. You never seemed to rush at eating your food like this before." She stared at me. "You know what, I think you're starting to look more and more like your father everyday. It seems like he's the parent that spat you right out of his fat stomach. When I look at you I see his smile, dimples and nose. What's next?"

My mouth hung open and the clanging noise that the fork made as it hit the floor seemed so far away. Suddenly, I couldn't eat anymore.

"Mom, the food was delicious. I'm kinda tired, I'm gonna head on up to bed. I'll see you in the morning."

"Okay, sweetie, goodnight." She sat at the table puzzled by my behavior.

I walked upstairs to my bedroom and shut the door. Minutes later it was happening again. I forced my fingers down my throat, ran to the bathroom, gagged and vomited. Tears ran down my face. I was afraid my mom would hear me vomiting and ask what was wrong. I cleansed my mouth with mouthwash and water, then headed back to my room. Looking up at the glow-in-the-dark constellation that my daddy had painted on my ceiling, I cried myself to sleep without a dream nearby, thinking about what I was going to do.

* * *

Arriving to school two periods late in my jean apple bottom skirt and lime green halter top, I strutted down the hall. Feeling much better than yesterday, I watched as everyone looked at me as if I was the newest student on the block. I walked up to Jessica and CiCi standing at the green hall lockers.

"Hey y'all, I'm back! What's up?" I said to my girls.

"We see," CiCi and Jessica said in unison, in a sarcastic voice.

"'Bout time you decided to bring your hot tail back to school," CiCi said, not knowing that I had been sick. "You've been missing all the compliments from them boys that always call you phat," she added.

"So, Malissa, what was this sickness you started telling me about yesterday before your mom took the phone?" Jessica curiously asked.

I was caught off guard by that question. As the words rolled off Jessica's tongue, I started sweating bullets. I forgot all about what I had planned to say.

Afraid to tell my friends the truth, I said, "Oh, it was just something common, I'll tell y'all about it later." Looking around at the number of people in the hall, I continued. "I don't want all these people knowing my business."

"Well, okay, just make sure you sit with us at lunch today," CiCi said.

Swingin' her hair to the side, Jessica said, "And we need to finish talking 'bout them bangin' outfits we plan on buying after school."

"Okay, see y'all then," I said and walked away.

I sat in my third period class trying to think up a good excuse as to why I hadn't been in school for the past couple of days. I suddenly remembered what I'd planned to tell them; that my mom had gotten sick and I had caught a cold from her.

The bell rang and I rushed out of the classroom. It was fourth period; time for me to meet up with Jessica and CiCi to go to lunch. As I walked down the hall, I heard heavy footsteps following behind me. Frightened that it would be someone wanting to question me about my attendance, I began walking at a faster pace. The footsteps got closer and closer, until I felt someone tap me on my shoulder.

I screamed, turned around and said, "I was sick!"

A puzzled Mr. Sholes said, "Malissa, it's fine." Scratching the top of his baldhead and handing me my notebook, he continued. "I have no clue as to what you're talking about. I only wanted to give you the notebook you left in my class."

Sheepishly I grabbed my notebook from Mr. Sholes without a thank you and disappeared as fast as I could.

I watched as Jessica and CiCi walked into the cafeteria with the two most popular guys in school, Rico and Ty. I definitely wasn't telling the girls why I hadn't been in school while those two were hanging around.

"Hey, what's good chick?" Rico said, in a deep voice.

"Nothin', what's good wit you?" I said, grabbing a red lunch tray.

Rico licked his lips similar to how LL Cool J did. He moved closer to me and whispered in my ear, "I ain't been doing nothin', other then thinking about how phat you are and how I'd do anything to hop onto that. I was gonna call you the other day but I heard you've been having that monkey on your back."

Angrily, I snapped, "What the heck do you mean by me having a monkey on my back?"

"Girl, you stupid. That means to be sick or to have some sort of disease," CiCi said.

"Word, for real?" Jessica said, butting into the conversation. "I didn't know that's what that meant. I guess we do learn something new everyday." She swung her hair to the side and pulled Ty over to go sit at the table to continue flirting. Neither one of them had any business sharing their fantasies with one another.

Ty was about 6 feet, light skinned, had a fresh cut, and was dating Burnside's most popular cheerleader, Naomi Scott. Jessica, on the other hand, knew Ty was up to no good and her boyfriend, Khalil, of two years wasn't having it.

I got my lunch and followed the gang back to the table. Before I could sit down, Rico whispered a seductive, good bye in my ear.

Breaking the bond between Ty and Jessica, Rico yelled, "Ty, come on, man! Stop breathing down that girl neck. We don't even belong in this joint! Man, let's go!" Slapping Jessica's butt, Ty got up and they left the cafeteria.

"So um, Malissa, what were you supposed to be telling us again? Something about you being sick and why you weren't in school for a while," CiCi asked, while looking at her monthly planner.

I felt instant sweat start to drip down my face and took a sip of my Minute Maid Orange Juice and threw up a finger as if to say hold on.

Bringing the bottle back down and placing it on the table, I said, "Oh, it's nothing important. I told y'all it was just something common." Scratching my head, I continued, "Um, my mom got a cold from God knows where and while I was home taking care of her ungrateful behind, she passed it on to me." Splurging a little with my lie, I added, "I had been taking Robitusin DM for a while and it finally cleared up. And here I am, back wit my home girls, all better!"

Both Jessica and CiCi said in unison, "Well good, glad to see you doing better."

"Anyway," Jessica said, "What's up with this shopping thing this afternoon? The show is in a couple of days. If we don't go today, I don't know when we'll have time to do it together because we have DECA meetings after school the rest of this week. And plus, my mom will have my car while hers is in the shop."

"Well, we can go today and hit up Scotland Town Centre," CiCi said. "They got this bangin' dress up in BEBE's that I want."

Noticing that the bell was about to ring, Jessica said, "Well, that's cool wit me. Malissa, are you straight?"

"Yeah, we can go. I already told my mom we were going," I said. The bell rang for the next period.

"We'll meet outside in the parking lot at 2:15 and move on from there," Jessica said, glossing up her lips before everyone parted to go to fifth period.

I sat in chemistry class daydreaming and thinking about what Rico had said to me earlier in the cafeteria. Did he really think that I was phat? Or was he just making conversation? Any other time he would have never sat around and talked to me like he had done.

When I got up to hand Mr. Nolesky my work, I felt as though my lunch was about to come pouring out. I grabbed a bathroom pass and ran to the orange hall bathroom. Tears streamed down my face. My stomach was cramping and when I looked in the mirror, it seemed to be even larger than before. Instead of vomiting, I sat on the floor of the stinky bathroom, blocking out urine odors.

The sixth period bell rang and I continued sitting on the bathroom floor until I recuperated. I returned the pass to Mr.

Nolesky and roamed the halls until eighth period. Sitting in eighth period I thought, *I'm not going shopping with them today. I can't! Just look at me, I'm as fat as all outdoors, and I can't fit a dress suitable for the Hair Show. Maybe I won't attend that either. I can't possibly go hang out with them and my body starts acting up. Jessica and CiCi would probably kill me if they knew what was really going on with me. That's it, I'm not going shopping with them. I'ma get my fat butt right on the bus at 2:15 and that's the end of it.*

I snapped out of it as Mrs. Shelton, my eighth period teacher, tapped on her desk with the yardstick that she could never seem to put down.

"Miss Tucker, are you alright?" Mrs. Shelton asked. "You haven't been in school for a while and here you are daydreaming. You're behind so I suggest you pay attention! Now here, complete these assignments. You have until the end of the week to do so."

* * *

Instead of telling Jessica and CiCi that I wasn't going shopping with them, I got on the bus and went straight home. I called my mom at work to let her know that I was home.

"I'm not feeling well," I told her.

"Well lie down," she said, in the most uncaring tone ever. "You'll have to make yourself a TV dinner or something because I'll be late coming home. I have a hair appointment."

"Whatever," I mumbled and hung up.

As soon as I hung up, the phone rang. The caller ID read Tucker, Matthew.

"Hi, Daddy," I answered.

"Hey sweetie, how are you?" he asked. "How's everything going over there? Are you flying down this weekend?"

Awww, Daddy! I won't be able to because the hair show I told you about is Saturday. You remember, don't you?"

"Sweetie, I'm sorry, I forgot about that. Well, you can come next weekend, I guess."

I felt bad that I wouldn't be able to see him this weekend, but I tried to keep the conversation going. Plus, I needed money for my outfit and hair, just in case I decided to go to the hair show.

"That's fine. So ah, how have you been? How's your weight?" I asked, trying to think of something interesting to say.

"I've been fine. Just trying to make it out here in the boonies. And my weight, let's see, my weight, um, it's all right but it could be better. Just got a little pudgier from not working out and eating all these chickens out here on the farm. Why you ask?"

"No reason. I've just been thinking a lot about you and tryna make sure you're in good health. That's all."

"Well, I'm doing pretty good." Then wanting to sound a little more interested in me, he asked, "So, honey, how you doing? Is all well with you? How's school coming along out there?"

"I'm doing my thing. I'm doing well in school and staying out of trouble," I lied. He'd never know the truth about how I was really doing in school because he didn't live near us and couldn't have a decent conversation with my mom. "I'm actually expecting to get the perfect attendance certificate on Wednesday. I've been going from the time the doors open till the last bell rings at 2:15."

"Lissa, that's great! But I'm not surprised. I know that you're a good child. Just stay out of trouble and you're going to make it out here in this tough world. You have a purpose in life. Once you find it, make sure that you follow through with it. Okay, honey?"

"Yes, Dad," I answered, a little touched by his words. My

mom never showed me this amount of attention. Encouragement at home was like every person in the world trying to succeed, very rare.

"Well, I gotta go sweetheart," he said. "Do you need any money for this uh, fashion show you're going to?"

"You mean hair show, Daddy," I said. "Yeah, I could use a couple of dollars."

"Well, I'll Western Union you $150. Is that enough?"

"That's perfect, Dad."

"Well, pumpkin, I'll talk to you soon. You can pick the money up after 6 tomorrow evening. I love you."

"I love you too, Daddy," I whispered, before hanging up.

I went downstairs and grabbed a bag of Oreo cookies. Since I was watching my weight, I vowed that I wouldn't eat anything heavy, especially with the hair show this weekend. I munched on them for a while before getting a glimpse of myself in the mirror.

"Just look at you, your stomach is getting fatter and fatter every day. I bet Rico really meant I was fat, not phat. But I ain't about to be exercising, I'll handle this somehow," I said aloud.

Something had to be done about this. I didn't have time to waste. I knew that if I were thinner, I'd feel much better about myself. I went into the dining room and grabbed the sales paper from off the table. I went back into my room, popped in my *'Green Day'* CD and looked through the sales at CVS.

As I scanned through the Health and Beauty section, the answer to my weight problems jumped right at me. Laxatives! They were on sale for $5.99. I'd get Jessica to take me after school tomorrow. My insides couldn't stop shaking from the excitement.

I called Jessica to make sure she could take me to the drug store.

"Hey, Jess," I said, when she answered.

"Hey, girl. What happened to you after school today?" she asked.

"My mom said I had to come straight home," I lied. "Did y'all have fun?"

"Yeah, we did. And we bought you a cute pink dress from BEBE. Girl, it's to die for!" Jessica squealed.

"I'm sure it is. What size did you guys get me?"

"We got you a three," she said. "You sound worried. We know your size."

"I know," I said uneasily. "It's just that I've gained a few pounds lately. I hope I'll be able to fit into it." I pictured myself trying to squeeze into the dress and my heart sank.

"Girl, you trippin'," Jessica said, snapping me back to reality.

"Listen. I have a favor to ask. Do you mind taking me to CVS after school tomorrow?"

"That's not a problem, Malissa. But we'll have to go after our meeting tomorrow."

"That's fine," I said. "Well, I have a lot of assignments to catch up on, so I'll see you and CiCi tomorrow."

It was almost 7 o'clock and my mom wasn't home yet. I grabbed my books to do some homework. Before she got home, I had fallen asleep.

* * *

I woke up the next morning to find a note from my mom on the kitchen table:

Dear Malissa,

You were sleep when I came in and I didn't want to wake you. Hopefully you ate. I went into work early this morning and since you were still sleep, I didn't want to wake you. I have a couple more clients to deal with and I'll be through with this one. Make sure you lock up the house good and turn on the alarm. If you're staying after school today, make sure that you call to let me know. Oh, and you're on your own for dinner again tonight because I have a nail appointment with Ann today after work. My nails look terrible. I can't believe I waited this long. Here's a dollar for lunch, enjoy. See you later, Mom.

A dollar! How could she leave me a dollar when she knew that lunch cost $2.75? I balled the dollar up and headed out the door to meet my bus.

Me, Jessica, and CiCi were known as "The Sparkles" at school. We were the most hated at Burnside. Today we all had on our vests that said "All you HATIN' females acting like you ain't caring, five minutes later, why you still STARIN'?"

I met up with Jessica and CiCi at lunchtime. They showed me the dress they brought me and my mind went back to the laxatives. I figured that I could probably lose some weight before the hair show even though today was Friday and the show was tomorrow. Any other day, time moved fast while I was in school, but today was different. It seemed as if time couldn't move fast enough.

We met up after the meeting and were on our way. I didn't tell the girls what I was up to. I just told them that I needed some sanitary napkins so they'd stop bugging me about what was in the bag.

"Girl, I hope you got Always because that brand *always* works!" CiCi laughed.

If they only knew, I thought. As soon as I got home, I popped a laxative into my mouth, slipped on my pajamas and went to sleep. I woke up every hour to go to the bathroom. The last time

I woke up to use the bathroom was 11 o'clock the next morning. By then I figured I ought to stay up for good.

Jessica and CiCi came by at one and we all went to get our hair done. By the time we got back home, it was 3:45. We had about two hours to get fly. I looked in the mirror and saw no change. I popped another laxative before getting in the shower. Jessica was coming to pick me up around 6:15. I hoped that Jessica and CiCi wouldn't notice my stomach poking out. I figured since I'd gone to the bathroom about a gazillion times, it probably wouldn't show as much.

We got to the Hair Show at seven. The hall where it took place was adorned with fly hairstyle posters everywhere. Since none of us had eaten, we went to a nearby stand to grab something.

"What do you want?" CiCi asked me.

"I'll take anything, except for anything wit beef or pork in it. I'm watching my weight. Anyway, that junk isn't healthy at all," I said, rubbing my stomach.

We ended up sharing a five-piece chicken tender basket. Afterwards, we went back to our seats and admired all the hairstyles the models were rockin'. CiCi loved the Marilyn Monroe hairstyle one model rocked and said, "Girl, that is cute. I would actually wear that."

"You probably would!" Jessica said, looking at CiCi as if she were crazy.

An hour into the show, it started happening again. I could feel vomit tryna come up and felt as though if I didn't make it to the bathroom, I would die. Suddenly, I couldn't hold it in anymore. It hurt like crazy as I made my way to the nearest bathroom. I fell onto the floor, doubled over in pain. Then everything went black.

* * *

"She's awake," I heard someone whisper.

I opened my eyes to smiling, yet concerned faces. The room looked so familiar; white walls, beeping noises, a nurse.

My mom, who had been sitting across the room, rushed to my side. "Hi, pumpkin," she said, stroking my hair.

I managed to muster a weak, "Hey."

"We were worried sick about you," she continued.

I sat up some to see. Daddy, Jessica and CiCi were there watching me like a hawk.

"How you feeling sweetheart?" my daddy asked, as he stood next to my mom.

"Fine, I guess. Why am I here?"

"Because I didn't pay enough attention to you, pumpkin. And for that, I'm truly sorry." Tears started to roll down my mother's cheeks.

Jessica walked over and said, "You passed out cold on the bathroom floor at the Hair Show. You really scared us, girl. When CiCi went into your bag looking for a pen, she found these." In her hand was the box of laxatives that I had been taking. My face grew hot from embarrassment. What had I been doing to myself?

CiCi said, "Lissa, girl, why didn't you tell us? Do you know you could have died?"

"What are you talking about?" I was confused. "I only wanted to lose a little weight."

"Honey, you were starving yourself." My mother took my hand and said, "Malissa, you're suffering from a disease called bulimia."

"Bulimia?" I had heard of that before, but I didn't know much about it. It was one of those things that I said would never happen to me.

"Yeah, Jessica and I have been doing some research and we came across some information. You confirmed what we found after you passed out at the hair show. Look," CiCi said, handing me some papers.

I took a look at the papers. They said:

Bulimia is an obsession with food and weight, characterized by repeated overeating binges. For a large number of men and women, bulimia is a secret addiction that controls their thoughts, undercuts their self-esteem, and threatens their lives.

These cases are also life damaging and need to be taken seriously. Although the obvious symptoms of bulimia revolve around food behaviors and a fear of gaining weight, bulimia is actually a way to cope with personal distress and emotional pain. Eating binges take the focus away from more disturbing issues, and purges are an effective way to regain the control and feelings of safety lost during the binge. Also, while bulimic behavior may have started as a seemingly innocent way to lose weight, the cycle of binging and purging usually becomes an addictive escape from all kinds of other problems.

"I-I have an eating disorder?" I whispered more so to myself.

At that moment, Dr. Joyner walked in. "How's my beautiful patient?" he asked.

Too embarrassed to say anything, I let my shoulders droop.

"Uh, Mr. and Mrs. Tucker, I'd like to speak to Malissa for a few minutes," Dr. Joyner said.

"Is she going to be all right?" my mom asked worriedly.

"Oh, she's going to be fine," he said. "With the proper treatment and care she should be in recovery soon. I just want to help her understand what's going on."

"All right," my mom said. "Baby, we'll be right outside that door, if you need us. You hear me, Lissa?" I shook my head. "I love you so much," she said, before walking out.

Dr. Joyner informed me about my disease. "You're not the

only one who has this problem," he said. "Your road to recovery is going to be tough at times, but you have to keep in mind that you can do it. You have a loving family and friends who care deeply about you. You're not alone. You'll be required to take some therapy sessions, as well."

When he was finished, everyone came back into the room.

"We bought you this," Jessica said, handing me a bright pink diary with the word "Love" emblazoned in orange and a pen that said "Best Friends Forever."

"This will help you to express your thoughts when talking to someone isn't enough," CiCi added.

"Thank you. I love you both with all my heart," I said weakly. "Y'all saved my life and I'll always cherish that." I reached out my arms to hug them. They leaned in closer and I kissed them on their cheeks. Turning to CiCi, I said, "For your research I still live." They smiled at me and took a seat.

Two days later, I was released from the hospital. Everyone was relieved to see me doing better, especially Jessica and CiCi. They had been so worried since the night of the Hair Show. Daddy had flown back to Louisiana and promised that he'd be back soon. Mom was by my side and at my every beck and call.

The following weekend after I was released from the hospital, Jessica and CiCi came over to visit. I had left my diary open to the first page so they could read it.

Friday, September 20th, 8:45 a.m.

Dear Diary,

I feel like I should have kept one of these a long time ago. I never thought that I would tell anyone the reason why I became bulimic. Honestly, I didn't see it coming myself. But this all started when my mom started telling me how much I looked like my father. I never knew in what way she was talking about, but the first thing I always thought about was his pudgy stomach. He was one of those guys that just seemed to easily gain weight. So when my mom told me I was just like him, I automatically thought I was getting fat, and was soon going to have his weight. But I can't just fault her for my insecurities. Those kids at school that called me phat didn't mean it the way I interpreted it. I had to learn from my ignorance that the phat they called me meant, pretty hot and tempting. Phat is also used to compliment a female on her body figure. So all along I wasn't fat. But I knew nothing about being called phat, so I turned to starving myself, which led to binge-eating, which led to impulse control. I actually hated it but it was what I had to do to love myself. But after all is said and done, I wanna thank God for talking to my friends, CiCi and Jessica, and having them to discover my problem before it was too late. I love them both so very much. Then I'd like to thank my mom and dad because they now make a difference.

My mom has quit her job, yes even before the case settled, to stay home to take care of me. She now works part-time at a tax office and has been paying for my recovery. I see a counselor three times a week, and I'm currently rebuilding confidence and eating without vomiting. My dad works full-time down at the Department of Labor. Oh, and did I mention that they're back together.

Yes, we're talking about my mom and dad here. They've decided to stay together for better or worse and through my sickness and health. I always wanted them back together, and look what it took. Dad exercises daily now and is cutting down on the binge-beer drinking.

Mom apologies to me everyday, and we're beginning to bond a little more. Both Jessica and CiCi come over every chance they get, ever since I started getting home schooled. Man, words can't express how TRUE they are. I look at the collage on my wall all day, which they made for me. They said it represents my BEAUTY. I guess it is true that everyone that GOD puts in your life has a place, whether good or bad. And maybe GOD doesn't put anymore on you than you can bear.

Signed:
Malissa A. Tucker
A SPARKLE forever!

SCARED STRAIGHT
by Lisa Williams

"Hey, Ms. Ford, when you get a chance can I get a grievance form? I need to write Mr. Goodwin up for discrimination."

Michael Goodwin was the Chief Detention Specialist, known for running a tight ship. I had never hated anyone in my life, until I met him.

"Discrimination?" Ms. Ford chuckled. "You just don't like it here, sweetie. You'll get used to it if you give it some time. You've only been here for five days, and I think you feel that everyone is against you," she said, touching my shoulders gently. Her lightly caramel skin tone glowed when her warm smile greeted me.

"He wrote me up, saying that I was horse playing. I was only tryna protect my walkman," I said frowning, while trying to look as angry as possible. In the midst of my bad boy front, I secretly undressed her with my eyes.

Over the past few days, I'd gotten used to putting on my game face. There wasn't much to smile about in the New Carrolton Detention Center, except for Ms. Dolores Ford. She was the Detention Specialist known for pacifying situations around here. Her measurements of 36-24-36 kept filtering through my mind and always brought me peace whenever she was around. A voluptuous black sister with the perfect body is dangerous for a boy my age. I was more accustomed to the fictional characteristics of the women displayed on my X-box videos than a live beauty queen.

"I'ma go grab that grievance form while you get ready for bed," Ms. Ford ordered, strutting off with her ponytail swinging below her shoulders.

"I wouldn't have to go to bed this early if it weren't for Mr. Goodwin!" I yelled. "He knows he shouldn't have dropped me back to Level 2. I don't deserve it! Just like I don't deserve to be here." I pouted as usual, but nobody paid me any attention. Not even my boy, Marco, and he's the reason why I'm here.

Entering my room, I started to undress. As I looked down at my blue jumpsuit, I began to float back into a state of depression. *It's the end of spring break*, I thought. I should be on my way back to school preparing for final exams, but instead, I'm locked up. I can't believe I've gotten myself into a situation like this.

Just four months ago, I was a quiet, 16-year old, ambitious young man. My life was so boring back then, I thought going to the movies was exciting. There was really nothing exciting about Bowie, Maryland. That's why knowing people like Marco had its benefits. During the week, I focused hard on my studies. I spent most of my free time pacing the perimeter of the basketball court hoping someone would invite me to play, or talking on the phone to my best friend, Sean.

Sean and I have been friends since fourth grade. He's also sixteen, except his birthday is two months before mine. I'm a December baby, that's why I'm so smart. I think the Lord sent me to watch over Sean. You know, lead him in the right direction.

Every semester when we both made the honor roll, we'd celebrate with an X-box competition and a root beer sundae. The National Honor Society at my school should've been named after me, Ricky Coleman. Yes, me, because I've lit that candle every year since the sixth grade. And now that I'm a junior in high school, I want recognition.

My studies have always been easy, but my specialty is math. I can figure numbers in my head so fast, that at times, I don't even need a calculator. Even though I'm good with numbers, people would still ask me to write papers for them all the time. It used to give me a sense of pride amongst my peers, and I had even begun to flaunt my services to buy popularity, that is until I realized they were just using me.

My dad, Charles D. Coleman, was proud of me and that was all that mattered. He knew I was gonna be somebody special one day because reputation was everything in our family. Most of our relatives are heavily embedded in law. My dad is the first Coleman to become a judge. Even though he doesn't express his goals for me verbally, I know he's not too happy about me wanting to become an engineer. And lately, I'm sure he's not happy with me at all. I'm surprised he hasn't renounced me and removed my name from the family tree.

My mom, Olivia Coleman, is quite different. Although, she's a prominent attorney and graduate of Spellman, she's more down to earth than my dad. She has a delicate way of inspiring me to take charge of my life while enjoying the fact that I'ma mama's boy. I knew at some point I'd have to transform and break free of her reign. I just had no idea that my life was about to drastically change.

* * *

Four months ago, the night of the Oak Hill High School game against Steward High School, everybody who was somebody was in the house. People sort of hung out with their cliques, just kicking it, not really paying attention to the game. The excitement was checking out members of the opposite sex.

I wore a pair of Ray Ban glasses, a button down, no name khaki shirt, and a pair of Levis. I've always considered myself to be average looking, priding myself on the legendary Coleman deep, cinnamon complexion. My dad says it's royal, but I'm not so sure I believe that. My physical features haven't changed much but my lifestyle has.

The night of that game was the first time I met Marco. He stood at the bottom of the bleachers talking to Jigga, one of the boys I'd written an English paper for. As usual, Marco was the center of attention. He didn't have to do anything special, he had it like that. He commanded respect.

As I walked by Marco and Jigga on my way out of the gym after the game, Jigga nodded at me nonchalantly. As I nodded back, Marco and I made eye contact. He just stood there with his hands in his pockets, instantly putting fear in my heart. Finally, he returned the nod. I was thrilled that he had even acknowledged me.

A week went by and I ran into Marco again during the 11th grade lunch period. He and his boys were dressed in all the latest gear. I couldn't afford half the threads they had on, especially the Redskin football jersey Marco had on. It seemed as though his entire outfit was perfect: a fresh pair of kicks, and the latest jeans and shirt. Whenever he and his crew walked past, people started whispering under their breath and pointing, the girls in particular. As Marco strolled through the lunchroom, I could hear the wannabes sending shout outs to him.

"Marco, what's up nigga?" one young kid said.

"What's up, Marco?" another curly head kid shouted.

Since I wasn't down with the in-crowd, I began to walk away shamefully. I thought I was dreaming when I heard Marco yell my name. I continued walking until one of his boys touched my shoulder.

"Marco wants to talk to you for a moment," his boy said.

I quickly turned around and walked towards Marco with my head slightly downward.

"Yo, what's up?" Marco asked, when I walked up to him.

"Uh, uh, what do you mean?" I stuttered.

"What do I mean?" he laughed. "I'm asking you what's going on. Somebody said you're someone who should be in my crew. I hear you're smart," he said.

A slight smile appeared on my face, because the thought of someone wanting me to be down with their crew was shocking. I had no idea how to behave.

"I don't see you around much," Marco said to me.

"I pretty much keep to myself," I said.

After about three minutes into our conversation, I noticed disapproving looks around me turn into looks of approval. The way Marco instantly transformed me from being chumped to being respected was impressive. From that day on, I was one of his boys.

I had heard a lot of good and bad things about Marco, mostly bad. The teachers and administrators often spoke freely about his class cutting and plots on getting him expelled. He had already been suspended a dozen times since the beginning of the school year. When Marco and I first started hanging, I often wondered how he could dress so nicely without a job. Not to mention the fact that he was 17, only a year older than me, and switched cars more than I changed my underwear.

I had listened to rumors about Marco being an enforcer in a local gang, but didn't know how true it was. I'd seen him and his crew jump dudes before, but that wasn't proof of gang membership. And I was too scared to ask him any personal questions. After a while, it didn't even matter because I was having the best time of my life. Finally being noticed and hanging with popular people was what I thought was next to heaven.

The best part of being down with Marco was meeting Shannon. She was the prettiest girl in our school. Shannon was sort of like me. She wanted to hang with the in-crowd, but her family was high-class. Her father was deep into politics. She and her friends would hang around Marco's crew from time to time, but she made it clear that whomever she dated would have to have it goin' on. But once I started hanging with Marco, she'd shoot me sexy looks every now and then. I knew I'd never have a chance with her, but just speaking to her is fine with me.

Hanging and cutting school with Marco had its ups and downs. At the time I had many regrets, but I'd overlook them. Man, the fun we used to have. Marco used to do wild, sporadic things, like the time we were playing basketball on the courts near the subway station. During the game, Marco was extra aggressive. He loved to dominate every situation. He dribbled the ball back and forth between his legs, showboating. Jigga showed off as well, but his game wasn't consistent. Me and the other guy on the team didn't seem to be getting the ball much and the game was quite tense because we were playing the boys from the projects in New Carrolton. They beat us the last time and that really pissed Marco off because he hated to lose.

Suddenly Marco stopped bouncing the ball and knelt down to fumble with his left sneaker. Everyone looked directly at him, trying to figure out what the problem was. His shoelaces were tied and everything seemed to be in order, but something was clearly troubling him.

"Marco, what's the hold up?" Jigga asked.

Marco stood, threw Jigga the ball and walked about three yards over to some off-brand scrawny dude standing on the sideline.

"Raise up out those kicks, punk!" Marco said, with a treacherous look upon his face.

The guy looked down at his sneakers not really sure about

how to handle the situation. His body began to shiver as he held his palms out, dreading what was about to happen.

"Why me? Why my sneakers?" he asked trembling.

"You questioning me?" Marco taunted.

"Uh, no."

"No, what?" Marco roared.

"I mean…."

Before the guy could finish his sentence, Marco was so close to his face their noses were almost touching. People watched from every area of the court. Within seconds, the guy knelt down and removed the brand new crisp Jordans from his feet.

Marco tossed his sneakers to the side and laced up his new white kicks, and everyone went back to their activities as if nothing happened. The victim slowly exited the basketball court barefoot and embarrassed after being played for his sneakers. Immediately, I felt a connection with the kid as he walked away shamefully. *That could've been me*, I thought. Not knowing what made Marco act that way because his own sneakers were practically new, my mind wondered momentarily. I figured I just wasn't used to this kind of adventure. Besides, I wanted to be in his presence so bad that I just overlooked the incident.

* * *

I'm not even upset about this ugly scar on my face because I got it having fun with Marco. I didn't even know how to ride a motorcycle on that sunny day in March when he decided we were going to steal four-wheelers from outside a local motorcycle shop. Goosebumps formed all over my body when I spotted the ATVs lined up perfectly on the sidewalk. Walking slowly toward our prey, Marco laid out the plan. Nervously, I thought about how I'd pull something like that off without getting caught. But before I could collect my thoughts, Marco and three other fellas ran and jumped on the four-wheelers like Speedy Gonzalez. With little confidence, I finally made it onto one of the four-wheelers. By the time the store manager made it outside, we had zoomed off like prisoners making an escape.

The thought of speeding through town and being seen with Marco got my adrenaline pumping. Unluckily for me, I was thrown from my four-wheeler trying to keep up with the crew. It felt like sparks were flying from my butt. Fortunately, by the time the ambulance arrived, Marco and the others had removed the four-wheelers from the scene. I thought I had been caught and forgot all about my health as the blood gushed from my face. That's how I ended up with the gruesome-looking scar below the left side of my lip. And even though this scar will be with me for life, I still believe it was worth it.

Although life with Marco had its highs, the fun ended when we got locked up. I'll never forget the date, April 8, 2004. I can still remember the events of that day so clearly. Even though I was mesmerized by Marco and trailed him like a baby pup, I should've been smart enough to know that a male dressed in all black with a hoodie meant trouble.

"Let's go have a little fun," he said, on that dreary day.

I remember that it seemed odd for no one else in our crew to be around. It was 3 o'clock in the afternoon, and we were walking through a residential neighborhood near school. Marco was acting really strange as he continuously slammed a foreign object back and forth in his hand.

"You and I are gonna go for a joy ride." He walked slowly toward a cul de sac off Route 301. The words *joy ride* sent chills through my body. *Stealing*, I thought. Immediately, I began to think of countless excuses to escape Marco's hold. I knew this type of activity was forbidden but I felt I owed him for letting me hang with him. Besides, he didn't have anyone else by his side.

Teenage Bluez

As we approached a black 1998 Crown Vic, my mind drifted. I had to prove myself to Marco or chance being labeled a scaredy cat. As he held the shimmy in his hand, inwardly I began to shake. He ordered me to stand aside while he worked his magic. I faked a smile like I was down, but secretly wanted to piss my pants. Zoning out, I thought about what was taking place, but hearing the locks pop brought me back to reality. Before I knew it, my body sat lifeless in the passenger seat of the black vehicle. The engine ignited and the stolen vehicle darted into the middle of traffic. Marco hit the pedal so hard the car jerked my body back and forth. Driving full speed down Route 197, Marco smiled.

Once again I felt like a punk because I had allowed a guy I'd only known for several months to psychologically drag me into a stolen car. Mentally, I could hear my dad say, "Son, think about it, is this something a Coleman would do?"

As we made our way near the Bowie Town Center, I wondered where and when this ride would end. That question was answered when a loud siren was heard approaching. My mind began to work overtime and my heart pumped uncontrollably. When the police cruiser pulled directly behind us, Marco looked at me and did the unthinkable. Instead of pulling over, he switched lanes cutting off an elderly woman. He didn't utter one word he just put the petal to the metal, speeding like he was in the movie, *"Too Fast, Too Furious."* Before I knew it, four police cars were on our tails like we were racing on a racetrack. I knew my life was about to end. Within seconds Marco lost control of the car and a loud crash pierced my ears.

Stunned, I blanked out momentarily and then I heard an officer say, "Put your hands up and step out of the car!" With their guns drawn and anger plastered on their faces, it was obvious they meant business.

Once we exited the car, instead of checking to see if we'd been hurt, we were thrown face down on the ground with my heart shivering in the bottom of my stomach. I could barely make out the conversation between the officers who were stacked in a football huddle. Whatever they were discussing, it was obvious my future involved jail.

As we were led away in handcuffs, Marco said calmly, "Say nothin' and don't let 'em trick you. Stay up."

That's when I realized this wasn't nothin' new for Marco. It was also the day my fun ended and I ended up here in the Wentworth Juvenile Correctional Facility.

Pressure on my kidneys broke my train of thought. I needed to use the bathroom quickly. I left my room and, upon entering the bathroom, three boys walked in directly behind me. One of them, a gigantic, hairy monster looking teen, grabbed me from behind. His cartoon character muscles sent chills through my spine. I didn't even have a chance to unzip my pants. What was going on?

Realizing the need to think quickly, I assessed the situation. *This guy reminds me of the Incredible Hulk on drugs*, I thought. I'm not even his equal. The only advantage I've got over this clown is that my eyes aren't crossed. All of a sudden his name popped into my head, Big Luda, the craziest dude in Unit 2. I quickly glanced at the other two boys who looked like they weren't sure about what to do. I panicked!

The force of his blow caused us both to hit the concrete. We rumbled and rolled, me on top of him, then him on top of me. I wasn't used to fighting so my punches were weak. I tried to pull a Mike Tyson and bite his ear off but, before I could, he pulled a move on me like a professional wrestler. Next thing I knew, I was in a headlock. While hovering under his funky armpit, I spotted the craziest tattoo I'd ever seen. It sat dead in the middle of his shoulder. Who would wear a man with a chainsaw chopping someone's head off? *Only a psycho*, I thought.

While taking my beating gracefully, I couldn't help but to reflect on the days to come in this center. Would everyone try to chump me? Would I once again be treated like a geek? The days of being ostracized by other teens were too easily remembered. All I wanted out of life was to be noticed and treated fairly, but instead I was getting my butt whipped. By now blood was everywhere.

Three detention specialists came running into the bathroom to break us up. As Mr. Goodwin dragged Big Luda out, his ferocious eyes met mine with an expression that said, "We'll meet again." I'm not gonna lie, I was scared straight.

"Let's go to the infirmary," a manly, female detention specialist ordered.

Although blood covered my face and clothes, and a stinging sensation wrapped around my body, pride took over my thoughts. Even though I was embarrassed, I wanted everyone to think I was okay. I had worked too hard at changing my image.

"I'm okay," I said, noticing several boys standing outside the bathroom.

"Now, it's obvious that you need medical attention," the lady specialist said.

"I'm straight," I replied, putting extra base in my voice.

"I know you're fine, but it's policy," Mr. Goodwin said with authority, as he broke through the crowd. As usual, things went his way and I spent the next three hours in the infirmary.

* * *

Several days later, leaving my cell, mental strain shook my body like a time bomb waiting to explode. I was on my way to talk to my lawyer and my dad. I knew this meeting could mean a positive or negative change in my life. Walking down the hall,

I felt as if I were having an anxiety attack. I thought to myself, *Somehow, someway, I've gotta get outta here. I won't survive in a place like this. Big Luda has me so afraid that I haven't had a good night's sleep in over two days.*

On the way to the visiting room, I was driving myself crazy with all kinds of thoughts running through my head. I thought about all the things my dad would say, all the questions my lawyer would ask, and all the facts I'd have to reveal. I wondered if I'd be released in the next couple of days or if I'd have to go back to court to see the judge?

In the visiting area, I was taken to a room off to the right from where the general population sat. The room had a glass window that was open to the inside of the visiting center. I saw my attorney, Mr. Schmitz, sitting there fiddling with some papers. I knew if my dad hired a high profile lawyer like Mr. Schmitz, I must be in some deep mess.

Mr. Schmitz hadn't changed since the time I'd met him at our house for my Junior High School graduation party. He was still sort of chubby with a circular face. Although his long hair startles you and people are tempted to think he's a member of Hootie and the Blowfish, this man is considered a white Johnny Cochran.

When I entered the room, Mr. Schmitz stood enthusiastically with his hand extended, while my dad sat in his chair with a frown on his face. He wouldn't even look at me. I shook Mr. Schmitz's hand and immediately felt relieved after feeling his firm grip. It was that grip that said to me, everything is going to be okay.

"Sit down boy," my dad roared.

"Now, let me talk first, Charles," Mr. Schmitz said to my dad. "We've got a lot of ground to cover. Besides, you'll have plenty of time for scolding."

"Carry on, then!" he said, folding his arms across his chest.

"Thank you, my good man," Schmitz gracefully replied. "So, Ricky, do you realize what you've gotten yourself into?"

"Yes Sir," I quickly replied.

"I don't think so. You see, sadly you've gotten yourself into a situation that will probably send you upstate for the next three years."

Hearing this, I almost fell out of my chair! My whole world had been turned upside down. The word "upstate" sent chills through my spine. I had heard from other prisoners that upstate was where all the rough neck juveniles were sent to do hard time. I knew upstate there'd be more Big Luda's than I could count.

"Calm down, son. You're sweating profusely," Mr. Schmitz said, resting his hand on my shoulder.

At that moment, I realized that my dad still hadn't looked my way. He sat calmly in his pricey Armani suit as if my life wasn't at stake.

"Ricky, tell me what happened and don't leave anything out," Mr. Schmitz said, grabbing his note pad and pen.

I spoke hesitantly, not knowing when my dad would eventually attack.

"Well, it all started when my friend…"

"Friend!" my dad shouted, cutting me off.

I regrouped quickly. "I didn't think he was gonna steal a car," I said, with a dumb expression on my face. "Before I knew it, we were caught. That's it. There's nothing more to tell."

"Son, that's clearly not enough information. We've got to establish a good enough case to get you out of here. Now, did this thug Marco threaten you in any way?"

"No," I answered, with raised brows.

"Are you sure?" Mr. Schmitz asked again, this time in a deeper tone.

Before I could answer, my dad's eyes met mine. They

screamed, *you better say he threatened you.* My mind raced for an answer. *There was no way I was gonna say Marco threatened me. He wasn't the best friend in the world but he certainly didn't make me get in that car. Besides, I've worked hard at being popular. Is it worth taking the chance of being labeled a snitch?*

"No!" I yelled. "I'm to blame for gettin' in that car, but I had no idea that Marco was going to steal it. I've got to get out of this mess. I will get out, won't I?"

My dad stood, his hands brushed invisible lint off his suit jacket. Mr. Schmitz gave him the eye, then looked at me sternly. It was almost as if they knew I'd be here for a while. Would it take me to put the blame on Marco to get outta here?

"I'll do my best," Mr. Schmitz said, standing and walking out the room.

"Is that it?" I asked my dad with my palms open, waiting for an explanation.

He followed Mr. Schmitz out of the room without even looking me in the eye. As the door shut, my nerves played an intense game of ping pong. I dropped to the floor, fell on my knees and began to pray. A few minutes into my prayer, Ms. Ford walked into the room. Her caring expression reminded me of my mother.

"You ready?" she asked sympathetically.

I nodded my head up and down.

Walking back to my unit, my attention turned from somber to roughness. I knew I had to play hard or I'd get beat down everyday. *Lord, get me outta here,* I thought. Before long, I reached my room, my temporary safety. As Ms. Ford prepared to leave my side, she handed me a letter.

Grabbing the letter, I took it from her and smiled. But when I saw that it was from Sean, my smile turned into a frown. I knew I should've been happy to receive a letter from him, but instead I wondered how many boys in here were receiving letters from girls and not from their boys on the outside.

When I opened the letter, it was just what I expected. So many words of encouragement covered the pages. Sean was smart enough not to write about all of the things I was missing but, instead, he wrote about what fun we'd have once I got out. When I read the part that said, "Keep your head up 'cause Shannon has been asking about you," I nearly hit the ceiling. *Why would Shannon be asking about me? I'm surprised she even remembered me.*

I lay on my bunk thinking about Shannon, my case, and my life. I told myself that things would be different when I got out of here. No more trying to be with the in-crowd because it has gotten me nowhere.

* * *

Eight days later I sat in a Maryland courthouse with my mother and father directly behind me, and Mr. Schmitz to my right. I prayed that before the court session began my mother's sobs would end. Her crying was making me feel guilty. The delay was killing me, but Mr. Schmitz said there was nothing we could do about it. Marco's court appointed lawyer was running late, and since we were co-defendants, we'd have to wait.

My nerves started to calm down a bit until I looked at the countless forms, transcripts and motions, being carried in by the district attorney, or the enemy I should say. I slowly turned my attention to the many footsteps entering the courtroom at one time. Before I knew it, Marco and his attorney were seated one table away from me to my left and the hefty prosecuting team sat about three yards to my right.

I turned slightly to get a look at my dad. His attention was diverted to the judge who had just entered the courtroom. Everyone stood when he entered. My dad winked at the judge. I quickly looked back at the judge to see if he responded to my dad, but noticed nothing. *Yes! This must be a good sign*, I thought to myself.

The court clerk stood, announced the judge and our case. Instantly court was in session. I tried to make eye contact with Marco several times, but he wouldn't look my way.

A lot of the legal mumbo jumbo talk, I tuned out from my mind. I concentrated on the demeanor of the attorneys. Mr. Schmitz seemed to have more confidence today than he did during our last conversation. Surprisingly, Marco's public defender spoke as if he'd been practicing for years. It seemed as if Marco and I were against each other instead of co-defendants. It all made sense when I heard the judge ask Marco whether his statement was true.

"Yes," Marco said. "Ricky Coleman paid me to steal that car. I wouldn't have done it if he hadn't paid me."

I couldn't believe what my ears just heard! Marco, supposedly a tough boy, was now putting the blame on me!

"He's lying," I yelled.

Mr. Schmitz's hand touched my shoulder. His demeanor remained calm. "It's alright son," he whispered. I turned to look at my father. He smiled. *I'm so confused*, I thought.

Finally catching a glimpse at Marco, I studied his face intently. Far from afraid, I mouthed, "You won't get away with this."

Marco gave a sarcastic laugh. At this point he figured he'd won the game. I sat trying to prepare myself for the punishment that Mr. Schmitz had warned me about. The likely sentence would be two years upstate in a juvenile detention center. I promised myself I wouldn't cry.

When the judge asked if I had anything to say for myself, I

said, "Yes Sir."

"You may speak," he said.

"Your Honor, I'm not going to pretend that I wasn't in that car by my own free will. I had no idea that Marco had intended on stealing a car. However, once I realized it, I should have turned away. Instead I didn't want to be labeled a nerd so I went along with the plan. I know this doesn't excuse my action, but I made a mistake. A big one," I said.

"Do you understand what the penalty is for such a charge?"

"Yes Sir," I said. Suddenly my mother burst into tears. "Will I at least get to finish high school?"

Mr. Schmitz's hand rested on my shoulder once again, while Marco's smile intensified. When the judge began to read his verdict, I completely blacked out like a zombie. I hoped after the verdict my father wouldn't disown me. After all, my entire life was being thrown away. Devastated and emotionally wrecked, I massaged my temples as the judge spoke. Unable to make out what he was saying, I focused my crazed eyes on Marco. Before I could get my thoughts together, two court officers approached Marco, cuffed and led him away. My mind spun like a world wind.

"What going on?" my Mother shouted, from behind me.

"I'm going home?" I asked.

"Yes," Mr. Schmitz responded. "Didn't you hear the judge? Son, you have a lot of community service hours to complete. You'll have to start that immediately, and you'll be on probation for six months."

"Yes, thank you! Thank you!" my Mother yelled.

"And don't forget about the punishment when you get home," my dad added, in his normal stern tone.

I smiled. "Anything you say, Dad."

* * *

Teenage Bluez

When I returned to the detention center to gather my things, I ran into Ms. Ford.

"I hear you're going home today?" she said.

"Yes, ma'am," I said, smiling from ear to ear.

"Well, I betta not ever see you in here again young man. Go back to school and do something positive with your life."

"Ms. Ford, you can bet I'm gonna be something great in life. I knew hanging with Marco and his crew was a big mistake, but my association with them made me popular, something that I never had before. But I learned that sometimes being popular can possibly cost you your freedom."

"You betta believe that. Now, get on outta here before they change their minds," she said, hugging me gently.

Swinging my duffel bag over my shoulder, I walked out my room and down the hall. Before walking through the door that would take me to my parents and my freedom, I turned around, looked at Ms. Ford and said, "You'll never see me in here again!"

After leaving the detention center with my parents, we went home. I can say that life after my stint in the detention center wasn't all gravy. Between going to school, doing my community service and doing time in my room, once again, I didn't have much of a social life. But I didn't care because at least I had my freedom. Shannon was really happy to see me when I returned to school and she told me that she'd wait for me until I got off lockdown with my parents.

I found out that Marco was sentenced to two years upstate and that his so-called crew never went to see him. You see, true friends will always remain by your side. Convenient friends are only there when things are good. Do you know who your true friends are?

IMAGE IS EVERYTHING
by Tamara Cooke

With 50 seconds left in the fourth quarter, the Washington Chiefs are down by four and the fans are going crazy, but the coach has a win written all over his face. The players huddle together on the field as the crowd waits anxiously for the last play of the game to seal their win. The coaching staff knew what it was going to take to get a touchdown, and that was their franchise player, Brian Kelick. He was 6'4, 220 pounds, with caramel skin and was really cute for an older guy.

In his pre-pro years, Brian was the star quarterback for UCLA and a number one NFL draft pick. He had been playing football ever since he was five, and it showed because he was one of the best at the sport. As a respectable franchise player for the Washington Chiefs, his fans idolized him and considered him a treasure. He was the reason why they'd recently won the Superbowl two years in a row. Football was Brian's life, second to me, Bria Kelick, of course, his number one reason for breathing.

Today was just a typical Sunday for the Kelick family. We had never missed a home game since I was born. I would be willing to bet that my mom never missed one even before then. My dad was her baby and nothing could stand between them, not even the groupies.

The center snapped the ball and a hush fell over the arena.

Teenage Bluez

Everyone, from the fans all the way down to the benchwarmers, crossed their fingers and chanted a silent prayer that Brian Kelick would save the day. My mom had her eyes shut because she knew if we made this one, we'd be in the playoffs. Which may not sound like a big deal, but for the Kelick family, it was.

A win meant more diamonds for my mom, more ESPN live coverage and possible endorsements for my dad. It also meant more girls for my brother, and for me, it meant another lecture and a bigger family name that I had to live up to and represent. Even though this was routine for me, I sometimes got caught up in the hype.

I looked around and it seemed as if the entire stadium sported Number 12 jerseys, and it didn't hurt that my last name was printed on the back in big red and white letters. If that wasn't an ego booster then I don't know what was. I looked down on the field where my dad was looking left then right. He knew he didn't have much time before one of those big defensive linemen would be all over him like gravy on rice. He spotted his man, Jenson, in the end zone and that's where he threw the football.

The ball moved in slow motion, then all of a sudden, Jenson caught it and the whole stadium became hysterical. Brian Kelick the hero! Outside of all my other drama, that really made me feel good because I was a part of him.

It was official; we had once again secured our spot in the playoffs, the fourth season straight. I knew this would be a good week for us. It always was when my dad won a game. He was the head of our family and, strangely enough, after a game his mood always set the tone on how the family's atmosphere would be for the next couple of days.

We gathered the family together and headed down to the locker room to wait until my dad had finished being interviewed and making small talk with his so-called friends.

Teenage Bluez

This part of the game irked me the most considering, once we left the stadium, we never saw or talked to any of those people who seemed to be so intrigued by our lives. I never understood what the big commotion was all about, because to me, we were just normal people. I had a few things on my mind, like getting back home, my last hour on the phone and my Usher CD.

As the players poured in one by one, they were greeted by wives, agents, girlfriends, and wannabe girlfriends, which in simple terms meant groupies. This part of the evening was the real nitty gritty, because I knew most of the players wives and girlfriends, so it was exciting to watch the players in action. The fight to get those men to the altar was like pulling teeth and I always had a front row seat with privileged information.

Even though I was a rookie at relationships, I knew enough from my parents and the after game soap opera to know the basic do's and don'ts. For one, I don't chase men, and I don't dress to disrespect my family or myself. Lastly, I don't give my body to someone who isn't deserving of it. I was only sixteen and in the 10th grade, but I had years of information pocketed. One thing for certain, I never wanted to marry a celebrity because, with the exception of my dad, most of the men were down right dirty and I didn't think I could be as blessed as my mom. So to keep it on the safe side, my rule was to marry a normal, hardworking guy.

* * *

My cell phone rang and I tried to ignore it, but whoever was on the other end was pressed. I reached into my new Gucci bag and pulled out my phone. I should've known that it was my girl, Tiffany. Though we're like salt and pepper, she's my best friend and I love her to death. We've been friends for eleven years. She's my right hand and knows what I'm thinking before I even say it. But believe me, if I had money to enroll her into a school of etiquette, I would because she's a hot mess.

She's one of those girls you can't take everywhere. You know, just like the guy you can't bring home to your parents. Well, Tiff, is an around the way girl. She doesn't get the picture just yet and I refuse to allow her to figure out this thing called life at my family's expense. I had way too much on the line for that. My family's name meant everything to my dad and he often reminded me of it.

"Bria, everything you say and do will follow you for the rest of your life." He would remind me of this whenever I went somewhere without him or my mom. I had to watch my every move, because if he wasn't watching, then believe me someone else was.

"What's up, girl?" I asked Tiff, trying to figure out what the emergency was.

"You still at the game? You better tell me whether or not you saw my baby daddy, Clinton Jackson. Was he looking good or what, and who was he with?" she said, all in one breathe.

Tiffany has always been way ahead of her birth age. You would have thought that she was about 21 or something. At the last season's home opener, this fool told me that she was going to the lower level to get pizza. About an hour later, the stadium security was escorting her back up to our suite. They told my mom that she was caught trying to sneak into the team's locker room. They were getting ready to put her out of the stadium until she told them she was part of the Kelick family. Man, you could see the steam coming from my mom's ears from having to claim this hoe as part of our family. This is why I never invited her to anymore of the games. I secretly called her a groupie in training.

Outside of school and my house, we didn't hang out too much. If my dad knew some of the things she did or talked about, our friendship would be history, so I did whatever I had to do to protect our bond. Normally, I would have Tiff's back, but her tryna to get with a player on my father's team was a no-no, especially Mr. Jackson.

Clinton Jackson was the new rookie wide receiver and, yes, he was fine. He was only 21, which isn't a big age difference unless you're under 18, which we were, then it becomes a crime. She was definitely biting off more than she could chew because this guy had a different woman at each game. This didn't bother me much because you're supposed to date until you find that one that rocks your world. But I knew better than to think that Tiffany had what it took to snag Clinton Jackson. So, of course, I ignored her request to hook her up with him.

"Girl, you trippin'. That man is way too old and he's got a swarm of groupies waiting for him. So, unless you want to get in the back of the line, stop asking about him! Anyway, you know my dad would kill us both if he even thought you were interested in any of his teammates." I thought about my dad's golden rule: It didn't matter how young, cute or single they were, players were off limits.

*   *   *

We finally made it to the car after hours of autograph signings, interviews and small talk with the other families. I had one friend my age at the stadium, Kelly, who was from Texas. Her father had gotten traded this season from Dallas. She was really cool but, most importantly, she could relate to my life as a pro-football player's daughter. I would talk to her on occasion but I never wanted to get too close, because like military families, they come and go. If your stats weren't the bomb, or you weren't starring on any NFL Playstation games, then you were bound to be traded.

Teenage Bluez

Kelly was very protective of her image. She made sure she used proper language, dressed like a lady, and smiled like we had picture perfect lives. We lived in the public eye and she knew not to air her family's dirty laundry. She was a pro at living the life of the rich and famous. I guess she was taught this by her dad, which was a plus for me, because I never had to worry about her doing anything embarrassing or ghetto when we were together. She was the perfect friend for me but she just didn't have the history or the love that I had for Tiff. If I could blink my eyes and trade bodies with Tiff and Kelly, I would be the happiest teenager in the world.

We finally reached our neighborhood after hours of traffic from the stadium. Rows of well-manicured million dollar homes lined the secluded cul-de-sac. All the players stayed in the suburbs of Maryland or Virginia. We chose Potomac, Maryland, which was home to some of D.C.'s wealthiest and elite families. Our neighborhood was filled with senators, athletes, prominent lawyers, fortune 500 company executives, and we even had a rap artist who lived two doors down from us.

Our house was pretty huge considering it was only my parents, my brother, who was 17, and myself. I often wondered why we had seven bedrooms when we only occupied three of them. But the older I got, the more I realized that money was power, and material things was a sure sign of success. That's why as soon as the rookie players cashed their first check, you betta believe they were at least going to cop a Benz and a Rolex. My dad always said that you can't take your money to the grave with you. For us, money was never an issue.

He had just recently signed a 5 million dollar deal over three years, not to mention that this was his third multi-million dollar contract. So, to most people, we had it goin' on. But to me, it was normal because this has always been my lifestyle. I never knew any other way. I guess some girls would kill to be in my shoes. If you ask me, my life was harder than the average teenager because I had so many expectations to live up to. At times, I thought *I* was the one out there throwing touchdown passes and signing autographs.

* * *

I awoke to the sound of the Russ Parr Morning Show. I looked over at the clock and I couldn't believe it was already 7:00 am. I jumped up because I didn't want to hear my mom's mouth about how I can't get up in the morning.

She would always say, "Bria, you've got two seconds to get up. You know I don't play when it comes to school. Now get up!" Then she would go through her regular threatening speech on how she was about to take my cell phone. After that, she didn't have to say no more, cause that definitely got a sistah out of bed.

Every morning she was like the energizer bunny, which was probably due to the fact that she's never had a job in her life, so she often over dramatizes motherhood. She would act like she had such a hard morning with us, and that she felt the need to treat herself to something special. She would take a trip to the spa, or buy a $1,300 Chanel bag for no special occasion. Wow, the mind sure is a powerful thing. Who did she think she was fooling?

The first sign of having a problem is to admit that you have one. I guess it's hard to admit that you're a shopaholic. My mom always stressed about a woman's upkeep; freshly done manicures and pedicures were a necessity. And a weekly hair-do and a personal shopper at Neiman Marcus would make any woman fall to her knees thanking God every morning.

My mother was a beauty even after having two kids. She was about 5'7, weighing 155 pounds, even though she thought she weighed 145. I love everything about my mom. I think it's the way she walks; it's one of those walks that turn heads immediately. Most people would easily misinterpret this confidence as conceit or arrogance. Instead, she's educated, sexy and sweet, all in the same breath. I want to be just like her with long, streaked butternut hair and all. My Grandma Jeanette named my mom Joy because of the joy she brought to her life. Amen to that, because I've seen a lot of joy being a Kelick.

"Thank you," I said to myself softly, after realizing I'd made it to the garage before my mother blew the horn. I hopped in our SUV and she pulled off like a female racecar driver.

Twenty minutes later, I leaned over and gave my mom a kiss when we pulled up in front of my school. I told her that if she came home with bags from the mall today, she'd better have something in there with my name on it.

She smirked, "Girl, you better get your butt in school and pay attention to the books and not the boys." I shut the door and thought, *she has got some nerve.*

I was always listening in on her and her girls' conversations about their days as single women. Sex and the City had nothing on them, 'cause my mom had Sarah Jessica Parker beat by a long shot. All I wanted to know is why she thought I was going to be any different. We do have the same blood, so whatever is good for her can't be bad for me. The only difference is back then she was only representing herself. Now, I'm not just Bria Kelick, I represent Brian and Joy Kelick, the Washington Chiefs, the NFL, and all the daughters of anybody who is somebody. If you haven't noticed yet, that's a lot of weight for a sixteen year old to carry.

Once I walked in my school, Tiff was waiting outside our homeroom as usual. We always had to approve of the gear that we rocked each day, and we both knew that we needed to be brutally honest with each other. There were plenty of days when

I would send the fashion police to lock her butt up. She was on point today though. She had on a pair of Baby Phat jeans, an off the shoulder sweater, and some new brown Uggi boots. Tiff's mom always let her dress very flamboyant.

A bit of jealousy oozed through my pores because, nowadays, all the *it* clothes were made for video honeys, and my mother wouldn't even consider letting me wear any of them. On the other hand, Tiff's closet was filled with all the hottest fashions, and her mom embraced the mini skirt while Joy placed it on the *absolutely not list*. I often wondered if my dad wasn't Brad Kelick, would I be able to show some skin. Although I wished I could wear certain stuff, I had boundaries for myself. I would take an outfit and look like Kimora Lee Simmons, and Tiff would take that same outfit and look like Lil' Kim.

She was born with perfect, long brown legs, average sized boobs, pretty skin, a head full of jet black hair, and she even had a lil' junk in her trunk. Which is probably the reason why I had all the fortune, but she had all the fame at Potomac Ridge High School.

In my opinion, Tiffany's mom, Gina Washington, was to blame for Tiff's current disposition in life. Her mom, single and unemployed, was the city's oldest gold digger, but she still managed to reside in Potomac, Maryland. Ms. Washington had been married twice and simply didn't view marriage as a sacred union. She treated it more like a casual prerequisite to dating. She wouldn't be caught dead with a man that couldn't maintain the lifestyle that was created by her first husband, George.

He was a sports agent whose clientele included top-notch athletes. She had given her all to the marriage, but unfortunately, her all wasn't enough to stop an affair George had with a woman twice Gina's age. Tiffany was the only positive outcome from their marriage. Everything else that took place only planted bad habits that would change her meaning in life forever. She was scorned and, like R. Kelly's song says, *'When a woman is fed up, there is nothing you can do about it.'*

With the help of a high profile law team, George found a way to swindle out the marriage without giving Gina much. After a long, nasty divorce, she was only awarded the house in Potomac and, between her plots to get revenge on George for leaving her dry, she had to figure out how she was going to maintain that big house. Gina's ego wouldn't allow her to move out of her house. She had been a housewife and she had lived in her husband's shadow for so long, that her only skill *was* to be a housewife. She figured, why not hook up with another rich successful man who could handle her lifestyle? Everyone needed companionship, so why not let it be a rich guy?

What she didn't realize was that she forgot the number one reason for being in a relationship, love. It's too bad that most daughters idolize their mothers, because this was the beginning of a disastrous cycle. Tiff watched her mother's every move and discovered at an early age, that the easiest way to success was through a man. Whatever it took and by any means necessary.

* * *

After four long periods at school, we couldn't wait until lunchtime. The bell rang and we headed towards the lunchroom. Tiff bumped into my brother, Brian, Jr., who was a senior and captain of the football team. 'B', his nickname, was very popular. That was because of the family name. All the fellas wanted to hang with him because his friendship came with lots of perks. They got to go to high profile football games, occasional visits and outings with other NFL players, and access to all the leftover girls he didn't want.

'B' had a couple of close friends, and even though he

wanted to be with Tiff, she paid him no mind. See 'B' was an investment to a smart girl, but Tiff couldn't see past today. She wanted the guy who drove the Benz now, not later. Gina had really messed this girl up.

'B' grabbed Tiff's hand and said, "You look really nice today. One day I'm gonna get tired of sweatin' you. I mean I've been tryna get at you for a long time. What's up wit' that?"

Gina smiled. "Thanks for the compliment, but you know you're like my big brother."

'B' was Tiff's wild card, so she played the big brother move on him to be safe. She had something up her sleeve; I just couldn't figure it out yet.

All of 'B's' friends started clowning him because he wasn't supposed to get turned down by a sophomore. I had to catch myself because, for a minute, I found myself copping an attitude. I didn't appreciate nobody playing my brother. I knew Tiff all too well and she wasn't interested in 'B'. She was crazy because he was a perfect gentleman, just like our dad. Even though he had a bunch of girls throwing themselves at him, he somehow remained focused. He respected girls and he really liked Tiff for herself and not her body. He had actually started liking her even before her curves formed. I was looking for someone that had the same qualities that he and my dad possessed.

I wanted to tell 'B' that he deserved better, but I didn't want to seem like I was hatin' on my girl, so I just trusted him to do the right thing. I was really wishing he would get with Kelly. She was the perfect girlfriend, but she didn't attend our high school. She went to Franklin High, which was about 20 minutes from our school.

We finished eating lunch and were on our way to fifth period class. Tiff and I stopped at our lockers, which stood side by side. She asked me to hold her purse so she could get her books organized. Her cell phone went off.

As I reached in her purse, I yelled, "Girl, are you crazy, you could've gotten suspended if we'd been in class! You betta be glad we stopped here first. Anyway, who could be calling you in the middle of the day? They should be in class themselves."

Cell phones were allowed in our school as long as they were silenced during class. If I used mine during lunch, I had to remind myself to turn it off before returning to class. Still digging through her messy purse, searching for her phone, I finally find it and the name Tony appeared on the screen.

"Tiff, who is Tony?" I said, with my mouth hanging open. I thought I knew all of Tiff's family and male friends and I didn't recall a Tony.

Before she could say anything, the phone stopped ringing. Her response had a serious delay, so I knew some bull was about to be told. This was the first time that she had kept something from me. As I waited for an explanation, I put the phone back in the zipper part of her purse. As I was doing so, my hand touched a slippery, small package. I looked down and it was a condom. Now this was double trouble. She had this embarrassing look on her face. The cat definitely had her tongue.

The fifth period late bell rang, so she played it off by saying, "Girl, I meant to tell you about Tony. We'll rap tonight about him."

Before I could say anything else, we had to rush off to class before we were late. My best friend, who I thought told me everything, for a minute seemed like a stranger. I always knew we were a little different, but now I was starting to think a little was turning out to be way too much. I couldn't wait for tonight's conversation. I was gonna be sitting by the phone with my popcorn and soda in hand. This was going to be serious.

Teenage Bluez

*   *   *

That afternoon, I rode in silence all the way home. My mom knew something was bothering me, but I insisted it wasn't. Did I really know Tiff? I mean, I felt betrayed and I didn't know why. We had vowed to each other that we wouldn't have sex until we were married. As far as I was concerned neither one of us had a knight in shining armor yet. Whatever happened to talking to your best friend before making such a huge decision? We were talking virginity here, not something like homework or a new ring tone. Who was this Tony guy? I had so many questions to ask that I immediately started to get a headache.

That evening after we had dinner, I heard my phone in my bedroom ringing. I almost broke my neck trying to get up the steps to my room.

"Hello," I said, out of breath.

"What's up, girl? I didn't see you at the game last Sunday."

Kelly was my girl, but she wasn't who I wanted to talk to tonight. I was going to have to make this real quick.

"Yeah, I was there, but my lil' two-year old cousin was with me, so I didn't get a chance to walk down to your suite. I was babysitting in our suite and tryna watch the game at the same time."

"Well, maybe we can go to the mall or the movies this weekend if you aren't doing anything," Kelly said.

"I'm supposed to be going to my cousin's on Friday night, but maybe next weekend." I felt so bad about telling that little white lie, but Tiff's drama and my friendship with her were priority right now.

"Okay, that's cool. So what's going on at your school? Man, I wish I could transfer there because nothing much is happening at my school."

Kelly just wasn't getting the picture, and I didn't know how to end the conversation without being rude. As a matter of fact, I wasn't sure why I wanted to end it, because Tiff hadn't even called yet. I was a little pissed that I had put so much faith in my so-called best friend and she was holding out on me.

"My Mom is calling me. I'm going to have to call you back," I eventually told Kelly.

"Okay, Bria, tell your Mom I said hello. Don't forget to call me back so I can finish telling you what happened today."

Honestly, nothing that Kelly had said was registering right now, because my main focus was to get off the phone and get some answers from Tiff. I was so preoccupied with waiting for her to call me that I finally decided to call her first. Normally calling someone when they said they were going to call you was a no-no, but this was an emergency.

"Tiff, I've been waiting by the phone. Why haven't you called me yet? You betta tell me what's going on with you!" I said, as soon as she picked up the phone.

"Girl, I know I should've told you, but I just haven't had a chance yet."

"Whatever, Tiff. You talk to me everyday, so you can skip the excuses. Who is Tony and why do you have a condom in your bag? And you better not lie either!"

"Well, let's start with Tony first. I met him at a party that me and Angel went to last weekend. I didn't ask you to go because I knew you wouldn't have been able to go. Your dad would've been asking too many questions. Anyway, the party was the bomb. It was nothing like those little fake parties at school. There were mixed drinks, older guys and no parents holding the walls up. Tony was there with his friends and it was love at first sight. He sent a drink over to Angel and me. He just turned twenty-one and has a body to die for. I'm still trying to figure out why he doesn't have a girlfriend. Since he's out of school, he forgets about my school hours, that's why he was calling so early today. I can't wait until this weekend when I can see him again," Tiff said.

I had to get my thoughts together before I said anything. First of all, when she mentioned Angel, I knew that was bad news. Angel was her friend from around her Grandma's way. It wasn't the best neighborhood or the best people to associate with. Tiff knew I didn't get down like that, and she knew Angel wasn't my cup of tea. Second of all, did I hear her say there was drinking? Last time I checked Tiff was still sixteen, and the closest thing to a drink that we had was a toast on New Year's Eve. Instantly I felt a huge distance between us and I couldn't figure out when and where it started.

"Tiff, you're trippin'. I know your mom doesn't know you were at that party. And, why would you want to hang around with Angel knowing she sleeps with everything moving? What makes you think that the guys won't think the same thing about you? Enough about lil' Miss Angel, please tell me you didn't sleep with that guy? You don't even know him."

"Nothing happened. He came over to my Grandma's the next day and we went to the movies. I really like him and he's definitely feeling me too. They were giving out free condoms at the Planned Parenthood Center, so Angel picked me up some. I figured that I should be prepared in case something happened the next time I saw him. Better safe than sorry."

I couldn't believe this was coming out of her mouth. It was almost like she was a different person. Angel was a senior in high school, and Tiff had no business going to a party with her, especially in that neighborhood. There was nothing but drug dealers hanging around there because Angel would always call Tiff and tell her what was going on.

As a matter of fact, Angel's boyfriend sold drugs and drove a Mercedes Benz, so it didn't surprise me that Tiff wanted to be down. She always wanted to be noticed. Yeah, it's nice to drive around in fly cars, but everybody I knew who had one worked hard for it. If she continued hanging around Angel, her virginity would soon be up for grabs and she'd be dodging bullets soon. From that moment on, I noticed a distance between Tiff and I that no one could explain. It was almost like Angel had stolen my friend and her innocence, all at the same time.

I could remember when going to the mall, talking on the phone about boys and stuff, or narrowing down our dates for the homecoming dance was important to Tiff. Now, the only thing she had on her mind was parties and this older guy. I thought we would experience everything around the same time. If I had to put my money on it, I would bet that Tiff had gave up the booty already. How could she? Everything we talked about was a lie. She was moving way too fast and, of course, I was the turtle losing the race. At this point, I didn't know whether I should feel left out or be happy that I had no part of the new life that Tiff was living.

* * *

My dad yelled my name several times before I answered, "Dad, I'm coming! It takes time to be beautiful."

I knew that if I threw that in, that would ease up the tension and put a smile on his face. I was always the last one to get ready whenever the family had a football event to attend. You never knew when the media or photographers would be there, so I vowed never to be caught looking a mess. Tonight we were going to the Washington Chiefs' Annual Awards event at the ESPN Zone. Supposedly, my dad was getting an award for player of the week. This was a big deal for him and he didn't want to be late, since he was the man of the hour.

I loved when the Chiefs had events for the family because they were always fun and full of drama. Somehow the groupies always found out the location of these events. The funniest thing was they would try and play it cool, like they just happened to be in the ESPN Zone on a Tuesday night. I mean how ironic is it that they have on their Sunday best and end up in a room full of rich, young football players? That's almost like hitting the lotto, and how many people do you know who have hit the powerball?

"Hey, girl, I'm glad you're here. At least I'll have somebody to talk to tonight," Kelly said to me, once we arrived at the awards.

"What's up, Kelly? Sorry I didn't call you back the other night, I had a paper due." I knew I was lying, but I couldn't tell her that I had just found out that my best friend had turned into a hoe overnight. I wasn't in the mood to talk. I knew Kelly was a good friend for me. She was a positive influence in my life, but I didn't want to give up on Tiff just yet.

Kelly and I walked around most of the evening, laughing at the players and their wannabe girlfriends. This was the best fun I had in a while. We played video games and she sat at our table for dinner. We even caught up on some high school news and talked about our plans for our homecoming dances.

My parents loved Kelly because she represented the ideal sixteen year old. She was moving at the right pace, not too slow and not too fast. She possessed all the qualities that my parents saw in me. They always pushed the friendship but I kept on pushing the Tiff thing. I mean I felt like I was her campaign manager, but somehow my parents never voted for her. They respected the fact that she was my friend, but she clearly wasn't a favorite of theirs.

My dad always said she was way too fast and that he didn't want me hanging around her a lot. I paid his advice absolutely no mind. He had some nerve tryna tell me who to be friends with. Especially when about seventy percent of his friends were living double lives with full time mistresses. I mean if he could have friends that he didn't necessarily approve of their decisions, then why couldn't I?

The activities for the night were just about over and the players who had families were starting to leave. The ESPN Zone would eventually turn into a happy hour full of desperate women and single players. Kelly and I looked over at the bar and glanced at all the ladies with either short skirts or skintight pants on. I had never seen so much cleavage in my life. These women were playing themselves so hard that it wasn't even funny. We both looked at each other and burst out laughing. This was the first time that she read my mind. For a minute it was scary, because I thought Tiff was the only one who had that privilege.

I spotted Clinton Jackson being naughty as usual. I knew Tiff would be interested in knowing what he was doing in here and with whom. I never brought up his name around her because I didn't want to encourage the crush she had on him. Clinton was a smooth talking brotha with a lot of game. I must admit, he was the cutest, most available guy on the team, and you could tell because the women were crazy about him. Whoever this girl was that he was talking to in the corner had really grabbed his attention. We couldn't see her face but Kelly and I made a bet that she was going home with him tonight, and tomorrow Clinton wouldn't even remember her name.

My parents were finishing up the last interview for the night. The NFL had honored him as player of the week, so he was on every news channel from the east coast to the west coast. Even though my dad was annoyed by all of the lights and cameras, my mom loved the attention, 'cause she would be the superstar of the football wives this week. There are some wives who never make it to television, so she was really living the life.

Susan Mann, the news anchor for Channel 5 Sports Center,

turned the mic to my mom and asked her, "What do you like most about being the wife of a star quarterback?"

She took a deep breath, showed her fifty thousand dollar smile and said, "Well, I love his passion for the game. Football is his life and through his dedication, he's been able to teach our kids to follow their dreams. He's a hero for us as well as for the fans. The Chiefs are lucky to have him because he's a wonderful father, husband and quarterback."

She hoped that she sounded educated, because she knew everyone would be watching. I smiled to let her know that she did a great job with her 30 seconds of fame.

I was relieved that this night was over. I grabbed my purse and, before I could get up, 'B' came rushing over to me with this look of death on his face. I was usually good at reading his mind, but this one I couldn't quite understand because he's normally the calm one in the family. Everything rolls off his shoulders, so I'd never seen him in a state of shock. As a matter of fact, the last time I saw him show any emotion was when my Grandmother died a couple of years ago. And I knew nobody had died up in the ESPN Zone, so I was really puzzled.

He grabbed my arm and pulled me in the corner. As he paced the floor, he yelled, "How could you hook Tiff up with that no good Clinton Jackson?"

"What are you talking about? I've never introduced Tiff to nobody. I knew she liked him but that's it. Plus, where in the world would she meet him at anyway?"

He pointed and said, "Right over there!"

I turned and couldn't believe my eyes. My heart dropped to the floor. Tiff turned out to be the girl over in the corner with Clinton Jackson. I paced the floor trying to rationally figure out my next move. At this point, I knew 'B' really cared for Tiff because his face was turning red.

"We've got to get her out of here, because if she's seen over

there talking to Clinton, then I'm in big trouble and so is she."
I looked around for our dad.

'B' looked at me and said, "Clinton is definitely going to hit
that tonight. I bet you he doesn't know how old she is." He
turned to look at me. "Why would you try and save her if she
put herself out there? Now, she has to deal with the
consequences. I thought she was different. I can't believe I fell
for her." 'B' looked like he'd just lost his best friend. "Dad
warned me about girls like her. I don't want people getting the
wrong idea about my sister, so I better not catch you hanging
with her anymore!"

"Well, I can't believe it either, but I'm her friend and I've
got to try and help her. Please don't tell Clinton because he'll
think I set it all up and my name will be dirt. God knows I don't
want that, because then Dad will be in it. You know he hates for
our family's name to be involved in any drama. Plus, he never
wanted me to hang around her anyway."

"Well, now you know, your girl's a hoe!" he said, pissed off.

Kelly interrupted to say her goodbyes. "What's going on
over here? Let me guess, a little sibling rivalry?"

'B' painted on a quick smile and said, "Naw, I'm just over
here trying to school my sister on how some of these broads are
too hot for their pants."

Kelly looked puzzled and said, "Okay, Bria, what is he
talking about?"

I didn't have time to explain and I really didn't want to put
Tiff on full blast in front of Kelly. Tiff doesn't understand she's
making me look real bad, but I was going to let her know once
the stove cooled off.

"Kelly, don't listen to him, he's trippin'. I'll call you later."
I gave her a friendly hug, just to remind myself that there are
some decent girls left in this world besides myself. I know she
was probably wondering where that hug came from, but I

figured I'd explain it to her in due time.

By this time, Tiff was exchanging numbers with Clinton. I had two choices, I could stand on the sidelines and hope nobody recognized her, or I could go and snatch her up and tell her she needed to disappear quickly. I decided to go with the last one, because who wouldn't recognize her considering the go get 'em outfit she was wearing.

I quickly looked around the room to locate my parents. I needed them to be as far away as possible from what was about to go down. Although they were walking towards the bar area, I figured I still had about three minutes to handle my business. I got angrier and angrier as I walked towards Tiff and Clinton. My best friend was actually rapping to this man like she belonged here. She even had this seductive lean like she was a pro at pulling older guys.

I took a deep breath and said, "Hey, Clinton, what's up? I didn't know you knew Tiff."

His mouth dropped open about two inches wide. I automatically knew he was trying to figure out the connection. My minutes had decreased down to about one minute, and I had my parents in clear view by this time.

"Never mind the small talk. Tiff, I need to speak to you now. It's an emergency." I grabbed her and, before she could tell Clinton that she'd be right back, I had jerked her through the crowd like a bad kid about to get a beating.

"How can you disrespect my dad by showing up here tryna snag Clinton Jackson? I thought we were best friends. Why would you put me in a position to look bad? It's obvious that you don't care about our friendship. Don't you have any self-respect for yourself? Let me guess, Angel brought you here tonight, right? So does Clinton know how old you really are?"

"Look, Bria, I'm grown and I can go wherever I want to go, so back off! You're just jealous of my friendship with Angel.

And I can't help it if Clinton likes me. I bet if your Dad wasn't some big shot quarterback then you'd be out there snagging you one also. See, you don't have to worry about anything; your future is being handed down to you, but my life isn't that easy. Now, let go of my arm so I can go and finish my conversation with Clinton." Tiff snatched her arm away.

I stood there astonished, trying to figure out what happened to the Tiff I knew. "Tiff, you can't go back over there and risk my parents seeing you. If they find you in here, they're going to swear I had something to do with this. Look, Clinton is talking to 'B' now anyway, so your cover is blown. Any lie that you told is out in the open now. You might as well save face and walk out the door. I'll tell the freak of the week Angel to meet you outside."

Tiff tried to hold onto her pride, but she knew it wasn't worth it. She walked towards the door, "Whatever, Bria, you don't even know Angel. And tell your brother to mind his freakin' business!" She looked embarrassed as she left the ESPN Zone.

For the record, I knew enough about Angel to classify her as a money hungry freak. I walked around for several minutes, tryna spot Angel so I could deliver the message. She was sitting at the table with Cory Randolph, a defensive lineman. Angel just didn't deserve a regular message delivery; she needed something special since she thought that was what she was. I double backed around the corner and found one of the team's security guards named Anthony. He has known me since I was a baby, so I knew he'd be down for anything.

The atmosphere had quickly turned from dinner to happy hour, so I could barely hear myself talking. I whispered the whole story and the plan in Anthony's ear and told him I owed him one.

"Sure thing, lil mama, anything for Baby Kelick," Anthony

said.

I hated when he called me that, but it didn't matter tonight. My name could have been anything. I sat back and watched the drama unfold.

Anthony walked up to Cory's table with this serious, no nonsense look on his face. He said to Angel, "Ma'am, can I see your ID please?"

"Why, they already checked it at the front door."

"Well, you look pretty young. As a precautionary method for our team, we need to see your ID. No one under 18 is allowed to be in the ESPN Zone after 10 o'clock. So, unless you can show me an ID that says you're over 18, you'll have to leave now."

'B' and I were falling on the floor laughing. My plan worked out good because Angel's face was completely red by now. It didn't help that she had to first pick her face up off the floor, and then walk by half the team escorted by security. She gave me the look of death when she passed me. It was obvious to her that I got her busted. Angel deserved a little embarrassment considering she just broke up an eleven-year friendship.

My parents walked over and asked, "What's so funny over here? Did we miss something?"

I'm thinking, definitely, but I said, "Naw. We were laughing about something at school. Let's go because I've got to get ready for school tomorrow." I really wanted to just lie back in the heated seats of our BMW 745I and decipher what had just happened.

'B' didn't even have to speak; I could read his mind. I guess this was a given since we were so close. I knew my friendship was over with Tiff. She was totally different now and I couldn't understand nor be down with her. My dad taught me way too much about self-respect to go out like that. I hated those long lectures but they finally paid off, because I couldn't find any rationale for Tiff's behavior. I used to think that he was worried more about his image being tarnished by my actions. But now I see that it was about our family respect and our legacy. He always said that everything that happens to us, and every choice we make, is a reflection of what we believe about ourselves. I knew that I had to make a future for myself, not just tag onto a man.

I always believed that eventually I would fall in love and get married and, as long as we both have mutual respect, commitment and love for one another, then I would be successful. My mom has always been big on self-esteem, which to me is a positive self-image. It begins with you and extends to all that you do.

I knew that Tiff didn't have any self-esteem 'cause, if she did, then she would believe in herself to get her own fortune and success. Sometimes I wished that she had parents like me 'cause, if she did, we probably would be at the movies right now instead of her being all tied up in this unnecessary drama.

* * *

Tiff was absent the next couple of days from school. Even though I was still mad, I was worried about her. Eleven years was too long time for me to just turn my back and forget about her. I walked out the side door of the school and pulled out my cell phone. This call was killing my ego, but I felt like she was in danger. Her cell phone rang several times but no one answered. I decided to call her mother.

"Good morning Ms. Gina, how are you? I was wondering whether Tiff was there. I'm worried about her, she hasn't been to school in two days."

"Oh yeah? I'm gonna kill her. She left here this morning

like she was going to school. She's probably with that scandalous Angel. I'ma find her and, when I do, she's gonna be in a world of trouble."

I felt like crawling under a rock. I wasn't tryna snitch on Tiff for skipping school, but somehow I felt like she needed me. She was the only one who could make a u-turn on this destructive path she was on.

Later on that evening, I decided to take a milk and honey bubble bath before I went to bed. I was exhausted from all the drama that had been unfolding these last couple of days. I dried off and climbed into bed. It didn't take long before I dozed off into my dreams.

Suddenly, I was awakened by 'B' calling my name. He said he needed to talk to me, it was really important. He had a look of concern on his face. I turned over and plopped my pillows behind my head so that I could give him my full attention. I was beginning to get worried before he even started to speak.

"I just got a call from Steve. He said he heard from some buddies of ours that Tiff and Angel had been arrested in connection with some drug bust in Northeast, D.C. They were with Angel's boyfriend and some cat named Tony. The cops pulled them over in Angel's car and they found drugs in the car." 'B' paced the floor. He really did care for Tiff. "The guys told the cops that Angel and Tiff were just giving them a ride home and they knew nothing about the drugs. You and I know that's a lie. Those dudes were probably making a delivery or something and didn't want to get locked up so they placed the blame on them."

"Oh, my God! I can't believe this. I remember her telling me about that dude Tony. She met him at some party Angel took her to. I think she said he was Angel's boyfriend's friend. I told her that Angel was no good for her and that she didn't know that guy Tony that well. Is Tiff still in jail?"

"I don't know, but dad and mom already know. You know how fast news travels around the neighborhood. You might as well get ready for the 'I told you so' lecture. Your friend is dumb. I thought she was smarter than that. She's out there tryna mess with guys for their money. Doesn't she realize that guys see right through women like her? Nobody decent is going to want her to be their girlfriend or wife."

'B' is messed up, I thought.

"They're just going to use her like she's using herself," he continued. "If you don't respect yourself then a guy certainly won't. Believe me, I'm a guy and I'm telling you how we think. I'm just pissed because I was actually falling for her. By the way, Kelly called. She said she would be over tomorrow night to spend the weekend since her mom was going to the away game this Sunday."

For the next couples of days, I got the heat from my parents. They lectured me until my face turned blue. Deep down inside they trusted my judgment, but they were just scared in knowing I could've possibly been pressured into some negative situations. But my self-esteem was too high, and I didn't easily succumb to peer pressure.

Even though I listened and sucked in all that stuff they were talking about, I really wanted to know how Tiff was doing. My dad said I couldn't talk to her, so I could only get the scoop from 'B'. He would give me updates because he knew that I cared about her even though we hadn't been friends since that evening at the ESPN Zone.

Tiff and Angel were found guilty on a drug possession charge. She was sentenced to 36 months; the first 18 months had to be served in a juvenile detention center. The judge suspended the other 18 months of her time since this was her first offense. I couldn't believe that Tiff was going to jail for something she didn't do. It was their responsibility since it was

Angel's car, and somebody had to take the rap for the drugs found. Tiffs mom was embarrassed and couldn't face anybody in the neighborhood. I don't know why she was embarrassed; she was the root of the problem.

I turned out my light and tried to sleep, but the tears silently streamed down my cheeks. I cried tears for Tiff because I knew she didn't truly deserve what she was going through. Sometimes the consequences from our actions are life changing, and this was certainly a lesson learned.

* * *

Over the next year and half, Kelly and I grew extremely close. I started to appreciate the friend that she was trying to be. Before, I was just so occupied with trying to make Tiff someone who I wanted her to be that I couldn't see the light. We were now in our senior year, and both of us were driving new rides we got for graduation. Kelly and I even applied to the same university.

I had always wanted to be close to 'B', so I followed in his footsteps and applied to the University of Miami where he attended. Luckily, Kelly and I both got accepted, because that was a long way from home, and we figured that we would only go to Miami if we both were accepted. 'B' had gotten a full football scholarship there, so I knew he would look out for us. He was a junior now and, between football and college life, he was having the time of his life.

Graduation day was just a week away for Kelly and I. We only had a few days to finalize our graduation party plans and shop for dresses. Our week was pretty busy and exciting all at the same time. We rushed to pay for our dresses so that we could make it to the airport to pick 'B' up on time. Of course, my big brother would come home for his baby sister's graduation.

I pulled into the airport terminal and there he was standing tall with his football jersey and gym shorts. He was the perfect athlete and somehow college made him extremely handsome. I mean he was always cute, but wow! I got out of my new BMW X5 and hugged my big brother. Seeing him I realized how much I missed his talks and protection. Kelly still had a crush on him even though she thought I didn't know. 'B' hugged Kelly, giving her an extra stare like he couldn't believe what a year had done to her. I must admit Kelly had always been attractive, but she finally started to get curves in all the right places.

The morning of my graduation was finally here. I couldn't sleep much because I was up thinking about everything I had gone through in the last couple of years. I knew that when I walked across that stage, that feeling would justify all the hard work I had put in. I pulled out my white dress and just stared into the mirror. It represented pureness because I had managed to make it through high school with my virginity in tact. I never found anybody that was worthy of my body, so I held onto it and it felt good. It also represented accomplishment. But most of all, it was a bridge for everything good that was going to happen in my life.

'B' opened the door and gave me a big smile. "You've got to be the most beautiful girl in all of Maryland. I'm lucky to have a sister like you. I thought you might want this," he said, handing me a letter and shutting the door behind him.

I sat on my bed and opened the letter.

Dear Bria,

I know you're probably surprised to be hearing from me. First of all, congratulations for graduating from high school with honors. I want to apologize for any hurt that my behavior caused you or your family. I always respected you and your family and I wanted so much to be just like y'all. Even though I teased you about how strict your parents were, well it was only because I really wanted to have someone who protected me the same way. I didn't have that in my life, so I turned to my so-called friends. I felt if I could get a guy to love me then he would protect me. I thought being promiscuous would get a guy's attention. What I missed was that those guys never had any respect for me because I had none for myself. I trusted people before I could even trust myself and that's why I'm here today instead of graduating. I applaud you for not giving in to the pressures and sacrificing your self-worth for attention.

At first I thought you just forgot about me, but you know I needed this time to think and get myself together. It has been hard in here, but I'm living my dreams through you right now. Yes, mine are on hold, but when I get out, I'm going to attend college just like we planned. I've been taking high school classes in here and I'll be finishing up soon. I wish I could be at graduation, but since I can't, I'll be there in spirit. Good luck in college. One day I'm going to make you proud like you've made me.

Love,

Tiff

I tried to hold back the tears, but I couldn't. I never imagined this day without Tiff. I folded the letter, placed a soft kiss on it and placed it in my top drawer. I could hear my dad calling my name and I knew it was time to head to the school.

By the time I reached the bottom stairs, my entire family was cheering and smiling. Kelly gave me a hug and we held each other tight. She was my newfound best friend. Her graduation was tomorrow, so the same support she gave me, I would have a chance to return it.

I watched the entire Kelick family in the audience as I stood to receive my diploma. My mom had tears in her eyes and my dad was all smiles. I noticed 'B' was sitting a little too close to Kelly. I smiled at her because I knew she had been digging him for years. They both deserved each other. I don't know what the future holds for them, but these last three days have been a great beginning.

I accepted my diploma and said a silent prayer for Tiff. High school was finally over, and it was the beginning of my career and my life. I had my parents to thank for molding me into the Kelick that I was.

The class president stood up and said, "I now present to you the Class of 2004!" We all stood up and threw our caps up in the air.

I looked up to the sky and said, "This one's for you, Tiff."

DOUBLE WHAMMY

by Leslie German

"Positive!" the words slowly drifted from my lips. At that very moment, I lost it. Melting like candle wax, I fell sideways out of the chair. What seemed like an eternity was only five minutes. That was how long it took the nurse to revive me. As I came to, I faintly saw a blanket of white uniforms hovering over me.

"You'll be fine, Niyah. Don't try and talk." I felt a soft hand stroke my hair.

"Were you able to contact her Mother?" a heavy male voice whispered.

"Not yet. I'll wait a few minutes before I try again," a softer female voice replied.

God, I feel so weak, I thought. *I need to talk to Denim. She's the only one I can lean on now.* Hearing part of the diagnosis confirmed I'd screwed up big time.

* * *

It all started on July 19, 2003, the best day of the year because I was finally turning seventeen. The newscaster said the weather would reach an all time high of 100 degrees. He was right because it felt like the sun had come down from the sky and gave the entire city of Philadelphia one big fat juicy kiss. I dripped sweat with every breath I took.

It was a tradition for Denim and I to plan for the big night. Our families laughed at how we treated our birthdays like they were a holiday. That whole day, we got divalicious, so that by night we were freakalicious…in a good way.

My parents were vacationing in Jamaica, so we kicked the events up a notch. Of course, they encouraged me to be on my best behavior. But you know us teens, in our world, being *good* really means being *bad*. Most times this caused us our own blues, but that's what we lived for - drama. Anyway, Club Palmers would never be the same.

Palmers' was the hang out spot for the "old heads." So, we really had no business there, but heck, we couldn't let our flawless fake IDs go to waste.

We got up around seven in the morning to make it to Peaz-E-Heads by eight. Denim, 5'4", 110 pounds, sported a tight spandex Baby Phat jean skirt with a bright yellow halter top that read, *Warning, Keep Out,* across her chest. That logo definitely fit her feisty personality. The chick was a born fighter. Although petite, her hourglass shape was the opposite of my vertical frame. Guys always seemed to be taken back by her big butt. My caramel complexion and fine hair got me some shouts too, cause I look like I had Indian in my family. At any rate, with her body and my face, we went together like Kelly and Beyonce.

"I want a dry wrap," I said to Denim, as we strolled through the salon door.

"Girl, get something new. Today is a holiday," Denim demanded, a bit irritated by my response.

"Naw, I'm gonna play it cool. If I switch up and don't like it, I'm gonna be heated."

"Well, leave it all up to me cause I'm going all out," she said, shifting her attention towards the wall.

The shop was the size of a matchbox. The holes in the salon

chairs screamed for a slot on an episode of *Design On A Dime*. I couldn't understand with all the business the salon pulled in, why the Asian owner never gave it a makeover. I guess she felt if no one complained, then there was no need to fix what wasn't broken.

"Oh, I see they finally took dem tacky paper posters of Aaliyah and Usher off the wall."

"Girl, that don't mean nothing. This place is still ghetto with a capital G! I swear if Ronda couldn't burn up some hair, I wouldn't come up in this camp," I said, sweeping my finger over the two-inch dust on the counter.

"Is that heffa even here?" Denim asked, with an attitude. "She ain't never on time."

Trixie, a flaming, gay stylist greeted us by the door. "Girls, y'all know Ron-Ron can't get up on time. But I'll get you started for her cause my first client ain't due to show until ten." Denim gave me a look that spelled t-r-o-u-b-l-e.

Trixie was cool and I don't have a thing against gays, but he, I mean she, had an underarm stench that could raise the dead. But today, we had to bare it because there was so much more left to do before the big night. I wasn't going to trip, but Denim was a different story. See, she had a big problem sparing other people's feelings. I begged her to be good and, to my surprise, she kept it cool. But I could tell it took every ounce of patience God gave her not to say something to Trixie. By the time Trixie shampooed our hair and took us from under the dryer, Ronda came strutting through the door.

Now Ronda was a unique breed. Let me see, how can I put this? She was contretto: country and ghetto. She was from North Carolina by way of Baltimore. She did two years at Howard before boredom set in and she quit. Then she went to Dudley's Hair School and moved to Baltimore cause she needed a change. Following some bamma, she found her way to Philly, had two kids and still wasn't ready to grow up. Now you tell me if that ain't sad for a twenty-five year old. On top of all of that, she lacked class. My mom said that's what happens to people who have a ghetto mentality; they grow up but never grow out, out of the ignorance that is.

"Y'all know I can't get my fat tail up on time." Ronda came in loud as ever, tossing her imitation Fendi bag on the console. "Okay, girls, who's first?"

"Let the birthday girl go first," Denim said loudly.

Immediately everyone in the salon, even the patrons, started in on the birthday song. Ronda's fat tail had to go the extra mile. She danced throughout the salon with a pair of curlers in her hand using them as a microphone. She looked like Humpty Dumpty's mistress. I swear I wish she had left those colorful Baltimore updo's in Maryland. They did nothing for her image. I was so embarrassed.

I smiled as I flopped in the chair. "Something different?" Ronda asked.

"Nope," I said. "Just dry wrap me like usual. I want to keep it simple."

"You got it birf-day gal!" she sang.

I sat back in her chair, loving the smell of the salon. The combination of the chemicals, curlin' irons and sprays took me back to my childhood when my mom used to have her own shop. Everyday after school, and even on Saturdays, I would sweep the hair from the floor. I even played secretary by answering phones and scheduling appointments. I felt so grown up back then.

The shop had rested on the Ogontz Avenue strip, which was the perfect location for any business. It attracted the right money making traffic. She made mad money back then but not for long. This gang known as the *Junior Black Mafia* quickly brought her empire tumbling down. They were these notorious drug dealers in our old neighborhood who demanded that my mom sell her shop to them so they could push their drugs incognito. She refused, and even though she fought hard to protect *'Cutz That Last,'* her efforts simply weren't enough.

I'll never forget that Monday night. My mother was kneeling down on bended knees, dressed in her satin nightgown in the middle of 75th and Ogontz, screaming at the top of her lungs. I had never seen her so hurt in all my life. The JBM had burned her shop down to the ground, and had left a sign on the curb that read, "I Thought I Told You That We Wouldn't Stop."

I believe that incident left a lasting scar on my mom because she's had really bad nightmares ever since. Lucky for those crooks my dad was overseas at the time because, if not, this would not have ended without bloodshed. See, my dad's elevator never went all the way to the top. I believe his mind was constructed for war. That probably explains why he keeps re-enlisting in the Army.

By the time I had finished reminiscing, Ronda was on the last curl. I took a glance in the mirror, confident that I looked good.

"Come on, Ms. Denim, you're up!" Ronda said, smacking her gum.

Denim was never in the chair longer than thirty minutes, because she wore her hair short and sassy. Ronda spiked it like Hallie Berry wears hers sometimes. We paid Ronda and headed for Denim's Aunt Shelly's house.

We waited on the corner of Broad and Lehigh for the 54 Bus. Lehigh Avenue was the Wall Street for all types of crime and corruption. There were crackheads who sold their bodies, drug dealers who pushed the crack that motivated the crackheads to sell their bodies, and the hopeless homeless who tried to find comfort on the cracked concrete. I was always freaked-out by the mean streets, but always felt safe with

Denim. She was my Smith & Wesson; she would beat some weight on a crackhead if they even thought about steppin' out of line with me.

As I stepped in the street to check for the bus, which was about three blocks away, Denim stood on the curb. The glaring sun blinded me and sweat streamed down my back. I pulled a clip out of my Gucci backpack to pin up my hair. As the bus got closer, we both realized it was crowded.

I turned to Denim and said, "Should we wait for the next one? I know how touchy you can be."

"Whatever," she said, rolling her eyes. "And nope, my Aunt Shelley is expecting us. Plus, we have to make it down to the Gallery by one. We can't keep Sung Lee waiting. She's got an attitude like a sistah. And I promise you if she jacks my nails up like she did last week when her man was acting up, I'm a hafta slap Mini-Ming Lee."

"Girl, you're sick." I couldn't hold back the tears.

When the bus pulled up, something inside warned me that we should've walked. After all we didn't have far to go. I should have spoken up, because Denim can barely stand someone looking at her, let alone bumping her.

Less than six people got off the bus, while fifteen more poured on. I was hoping that my hair wouldn't sweat out, which was really the least of my concerns, considering Denim's bad temper. I wasn't the fighting type; I left that to her and my dad. Once we got on, I led the way towards the back of the bus. Rosa Parks wouldn't be happy about this, but heck, we were all Black up in there.

"You betta watch my feet," I heard a woman's voice say.

I was from Mount Airy and wasn't use to the roughness of North Philly women. They were visibly the roughest in the city. I thought, *Please don't let that be Denim she's talking to.* As I slowly turned, peering over my shoulder, I saw the angry look on Denim's face. *My God,* I thought, *not today.*

"Look you old hag, if ya corns weren't so big…"

Before Denim could finish her sentence, the woman had jumped to her feet and was standing in her face. They stood nose to nose in the middle of the aisle, like two stars on Celebrity Death Match. It was funny how all of a sudden space became available. With my left hand, I yanked Denim by her halter strings, nearly choking her.

"Alright, Denim," I calmly said, so that she wouldn't flip out on me.

Before I knew it, the thirty-something year old woman swung a left hook at Denim's head. As big as she was, her name should have been Big Bertha. I grabbed Denim just in time to avoid her from being lumped up. There was no way she would have survived that blow. She was tough but not that tough.

"Oh, hell no, let me at that old bitty!" Denim screamed, charging at the woman's neck.

"Would y'all hoochies sit down so we can take off!" a male voice sounded from the front of the bus.

Both Denim and the woman froze like fighters in the Matrix.

"Who you callin' a hoochie?" they said, turning their attention towards the name caller in the front. "We'll both come up there and kick your tail!" the woman yelled, proud of her missing front tooth.

"Yeah, Miss, I know that's right," Denim chimed in.

I tell you some people in this world are just plain dysfunctional, and my best friend, Denim, was no exception. She was a definite patient for a head doctor.

The SEPTA driver sped off. *Thank God we're only a few stops away,* I thought. As we stepped off the bus at Dobbins High School at 22nd and Lehigh, I looked at Denim and shook my head.

"I was getting ready to do damage to that old broad," she bragged, after we had gotten off the bus.

"Whatever tough Tony. You were about to get an old-school beat down," I joked.

I took two steps and Denim stuck her foot out trying to trip me up, but I was too quick. I positioned my hands for a battle.

"Alright, now don't get a Mount Airy beat down," I said, laughing.

"Please, believe me you don't want none of this." She stepped in my direction. We joked until we reached the store on the corner just before Aunt Shelley's block. A little more than halfway down the street, Denim took off running.

"What are you doing?" I yelled. "We're almost there."

"Girl, I gotta…," she said, running up her Aunt's steps.

Denim always had to go to the bathroom. I think she had a serious medical condition, but refused to admit it. She banged on the door like a mad woman. Aunt Shelley slung the screen door wide open, holding a steel bat in her hand. Denim practically knocked her down.

"Let me guess, she's got to clean out her darn colon?" Aunt Shelly asked me, as I followed her in the house.

"Yup, you got it Aunt Shelley."

"I hear y'all talking about me down there!" Denim yelled from the bathroom.

"Just get down here dooky, girl," Aunt Shelley joked.

Aunt Shelley was crazy. Every other word that came out of her mouth was some cuss word or funny saying. People didn't expect her to be as wise as she was because she looked so young. She was well into her late thirties, but dressed like the young girls. Her five kids had different baby daddies, but that never stopped her from gettin' her swerve on.

Despite having to care for so many children, she gave Denim the world. She loved her like she was her own and not her brother's child. She always showed Denim love by fussing. I personally lived for her fried chicken, rice and vegetarian beans.

"Where y'all heffas been? Denim, you know I gotta go straighten out the money on my Access account. Uncle Sam keeps screwing up my cash," she said, as Denim came down the steps. "And I swear I don't want to get locked down for kung fuin' the President."

"Aunt Shelley, I almost had to steal this chick on the bus," Denim said, changing the subject.

Aunt Shelley rolled her eyes. "Did you wash your hands, nasty?"

"Yeah."

"And what do you mean by almost? Didn't I tell you to kick butt and take names? I don't wanna hear nothin' about what you coulda, shoulda, woulda done. Chick, you didn't, so I'm turning a deaf ear on you Tyra Banks wannabe."

Denim looked over at me as if to say, *'Ooh, I just want one day to steal her.'* But she knew that if she wanted to live to see her next birthday, she would have to bite her tongue. Aunt Shelley wasn't one to be played with. She could make the devil cry out for the Lord.

* * *

An hour before we left for the party, the thrill was thick in the air. As we finished making the final make-up touches, Denim and I looked at each other with excitement.

"Step back, girl! Dang, if I were a guy, I'd talk to me," I said, glancing at myself in the mirror.

"What about me? Would you hit on me if you were a guy?" Denim asked, brushing her hips.

"Diva, get over yourself. It's not that serious." I nudged her shoulder.

"Heck if it ain't. I'm fantabulous!"

"No, you are c-r-a-z-y. But I must admit by the looks of things, I'd definitely talk to me," I said, swaying my booty in the mirror. We laughed like two eight-year olds.

As I took one step down the stairs, the bell rang. Aaron says we're never ready, but this time he was going to be truly surprised. Aaron was one of Denim's older friends who we relied on for rides. He liked Denim a lot, but she wasn't feelin' him like that. She said he didn't possess enough thug-ism. I personally thought he was cool and fine, to say the least. He put me in the mind of a shorter Kobe Bryant, minus his doggish ways.

"Hey, Aaron," I cheesed as he came inside, heading straight for the kitchen like he always did.

"What up, Niyah?" He didn't even look my way. "What y'all got to drink up in here?"

I ignored him, admiring his Gucci loafers. "Where'd you get those Gucci's?"

"Come on now, girl, you know players never reveal their fashion secrets. Just call me, *the man*, and we'll leave it at that." He opened the frig and took out the Sierra Mist. "Let's focus on whether or not you chicken heads are ready to go," he said, drinking straight from the bottle. "Where's the prima donna?"

"I heard that," Denim said, as she pranced into the kitchen. "The queen is here, so let the party begin." We both eyed her like she had two heads.

"It's definitely time to roll," Aaron said. "She's ready for an audience."

"Dang, Aaron, you didn't even wish me a happy birthday," I said.

"What!" Denim said, slinging her head around.

I tried to lighten things up by throwing Aaron a slight grin.

I knew Denim was prepared to bite of his head. He gave me a frown in return for my smile. I felt bad.

"Your gift is in the car." He snatched his keys from the table and slammed the screen door behind him. Denim gazed at me without a care.

* * *

As we pulled up in front of Club Palmers, I clipped the rhinestone necklace that Aaron gave me around my neck. I thanked him with a kiss. When I saw that the line into the club wrapped around the block, I got hyped.

"Whew, we're gonna have a bangin' time tonight!" Denim screamed out the window, eying all the men who lined the row of cars parked in the middle of Spring Garden Street. "Dang, Niyah, do you see all the brothers?"

I could tell Aaron was heated by her comment, so I watched his every move. "Um hum," was all I managed to muster. But I felt the excitement in my bones.

I looked so good in my fitted DKNY dragon printed jeans and red Prada camisole top, that I knew tonight I'd meet a man. As we strutted down the sidewalk, I caught the eye of a curly haired cute guy. He smiled at me like I was a Krispy Creme Donut.

"Girl, did you see the way he looked at you?" Denim said.

"I *did*," Aaron said. "You better chill, girl, he looks like danger."

I can handle myself, I thought. And cutie was definitely worth a try.

The line moved quickly. There were about ten people in front of us and I began to get nervous. Although our IDs were done by Skeeter, the best crook in West Philly, I couldn't help but think about the embarrassment I'd feel if we got caught.

"Step forward and have your IDs ready!" the burly bodyguard yelled.

I'd hate to get him mad, I thought. He was a toss up between D-Boe and Suge Knight. Aaron went first.

Aaron handed the man his ID. "Step aside, sir. We need to pat you down for weapons." He directed Aaron to the left.

Oh God, where are we going to a party or a prison? I wondered.

"IDs ladies."

Denim presented hers as if she dared him to question her age. He looked closely at her and then at the picture.

"When's your birthday?" he questioned. I was so scared I started to sweat under my armpits. I began to do the math in my head.

"August 9, 1982," Denim blurted out.

The big guy studied Denim from head to toe. "I smell Similac," he said. The partygoers behind us burst out into laughter. "Are you sure you're twenty-one?"

I saw the horns growing out of Denim's head; she had no respect when it came to people she didn't know. "Look, man, I want to get my party on. Are you gonna let me in or what?"

"Oh, I see you got a little spunk," he smiled.

In the midst of all the drama, poor Aaron stood in the vestibule shaking his head. His face was filled with so much fear he could have pooped his pants. Nervous, he stepped slightly to the side, and I saw the same guy from the line staring at me. It was kind of freaky because it was as if he'd timed his wait.

"Okay, little mamma, you're clear," the bodyguard chuckled.

Denim snatched her ID out of his hand and switched towards the female officer awaiting her. I saw the cop make her empty all the contents from her purse. I was so afraid because I always kept an emergency girly pack in the zipper part of my bag. To my surprise, the guard checked my information and let me right through.

"Open your purse," the cop told me. Thank goodness she didn't force me to empty my bag. "Okay," she said, as she looked at me real strange. I ignored her and kept moving. We were all relieved.

"You would think we were trying to get into the White House," Denim screamed, over top of the music.

"I'ma have to leave you two home until you're of legal age," Aaron sighed, as he checked his gear in the mirror.

"Whatever." I took in the environment.

Palmers was nothing like I had expected. We had to climb up a long set of dark, narrow stairs just to get to the first dance floor. There was just enough space for one single line of people to pass. The blue carpet that lined the floor was nicely padded under our feet. At the top of the first level, the DJ was mixing the Caribbean sounds of Buju Bonton and Elephant Man. It was packed, so much so, it made me nervous. If anything jumped off, I would have nowhere to run. We pushed our way to the edge of the dance floor.

"Do you want to dance?" Aaron asked Denim. She swayed her hips to the music.

"Yeah, come on," she said.

They left me standing alone, and I took that time to check around for an escape route. Suddenly I felt a light air blowing on the back of my neck. I was too afraid to turn around, but when a set of hands rested on my lower back like they were supposed to be there, it left me no choice.

"Hey, sexy," I heard the mellow voice say. His words melted my heart. I turned my head slowly and stared up at the eyes of the cutie from the line. I didn't know if I should smile or melt, so I smiled.

"Oh, thank you," I said. I turned my body to face him. He

took hold of my hand and led me to a quiet space outside of the Reggae Room.

"Wait, I need to tell my friends where I'm going," I tried to yell over the music. He totally ignored me.

"What's your name?" he said, as he sat me down on the bench.

"My name is Niyah, and yours?"

"I'm Malik, your new man." He swept the bottom of my chin with his hand. I felt tingly inside.

"Hey, Malik," a very attractive woman spoke as she passed by. He didn't flinch. He looked deep into my eyes like I was the only woman there.

"So, where you live, baby girl?"

"Mount Airy," I answered, sweeping my hair to the side.

"What in the hell are you doing, Niyah?" I heard Denim's voice yell from across the room. She stormed straight in our direction. "I've been going crazy looking for you. Why did you leave without telling me where you were going?"

"Are you her girl or her girlfriend?" Malik intervened.

"Who in the hell are you?" Denim growled, clutching my hand.

For the first time I had hit it big. Not only was he fine, he was older than me. And the way his green eyes glowed in the dark, there was no way on earth I could let him get away. This was an opportunity of a lifetime, and I didn't want her to mess it up for me.

"Look, Denim," I said, "you and Aaron can go. I'll catch up with y'all later. I'm a big girl, I can handle myself."

Malik looked at Aaron as if to size him up, but Aaron being the nice guy that he was didn't flinch. Malik stepped directly in front of Denim. I took a deep breath, afraid of the stirring drama.

"She said she's cool," Malik said. A drop of spit landed on

Denim's nose.

"Yo, you better take a tic-tac and two steps back!" she yelled, prepared to fight.

A crowd began to form in the small space. Denim looked at me as if to say, *Are you coming or not?* I was thinking, *or not.* I really felt like I was stuck between Biggie and Tupac. It was tight for me to be chillin' with a baller. Denim was my girl and all, but I needed a change of pace. I turned toward Malik and Denim knew my answer; that I wasn't going with them.

"Alright, but are you sure this is what you want?" she asked. I shook my head like a guilty two-year old.

Denim looked at her watch. "You better be at the front door by one or I'm gonna get postal up in here." She looked Malik dead in the face as she pushed Aaron to the side, before disappearing into the crowd. Aaron followed her shaking his head in shame. People stared, but I didn't care, it was none of their business.

"Look, Ma, where were we before Whitney Houston came with her drama?" Malik said, totally dismissing the staring crowd.

"I don't know why my girl trips like that."

"She needs to be dealt with." I bet that hoe don't even have a man."

"As a matter of fact she doesn't." I felt awful for saying that, but it was already out and I couldn't take it back.

Although I felt that he'd gone too far, I didn't entertain the idea of saying so. His six-pack put me on dumb-dumb mode. Denim does need to find her place and stay in it sometimes. Before I knew it, a sweet taste from his tongue met mine. *Oh snap*, I thought, *not right in the middle of my thought. What drink was that?* Honestly it felt good, but I yanked back.

"Whoa, what are you doing?" I asked.

"Look, Ma, I'm a grown man. I don't have time for games.

Your lips are juicy and I want to enjoy them. If you can't handle a simple kiss, then let me know now." He moved in closer for another one before I could respond.

"Naw, it's cool," I said. "You threw me off guard that's all."

I didn't want him to know how young I really was so I played like it was no big deal. It was a bit much for me, because I was still a virgin. I had only kissed two boys in my life, but not that passionately. Let me see; there was Darrell in the fifth grade and Brandon in the tenth. I was real inexperienced.

Denim and I promised not to lose our virginity until we got married. But whatever Malik was working with made me feel good, so good that it frightened me. My body felt something it hadn't before. It was as if he had awakened something inside me that was dead.

We talked and kissed, and kissed and talked some more for the rest of the night. I found out that he was twenty-three years old, and had fathered a child at nineteen. That made me uneasy, but he said that the baby's mamma was no longer in the picture. Malik also told me that his mother was raising his little girl because he worked long hours and couldn't care for her like the courts wanted him to. He said that he was looking for a wife and that I was a sure 'nuff candidate. He said all the right things. I blushed all night.

I met Denim and Aaron at the front of the club at 1 o'clock like she ordered. It was so hard for me to tear myself away from Malik, but I told him if he let me go that I'd see him the next day. He agreed.

"I'm not going to even trip off of Mr. Green Eyes, but I don't like his style," Denim said, once we were on our way home. She turned to Aaron for support, but he kept looking straight ahead at the road.

"Look, Denim, he's really cool. You just have to get to know him," I told her.

"Whatever! I don't care what you say, that dude is no good for you."

This time I wasn't willing to go there with her. Denim always had a very strong opinion about things, but right now I wasn't the least bit interested in her thoughts. I liked this guy and I wasn't going to let her interfere with that. Maybe she was just jealous.

I was glad when we reached my front door. I got tired of the silence all the way home. I said my good-byes and hopped out of the car. I closed the door and threw my keys on the table. Sleep and Malik were all I wanted.

*   *   *

When I woke up the next morning, I smelled french toast and bacon coming from the kitchen. *My mom must be home,* I thought. I rolled out of bed and slid into my Tommy Hillfiger thong slippers and snatched my robe from the closet hook. After I brushed my teeth, I ran downstairs in anticipation of seeing my parents.

"Oh, my God!" I yelled as I reached the bottom of the stairs. To my surprise, Malik was standing in my kitchen cooking.

"Good morning, beautiful," he said. "Did you sleep well?"

"What in the world are you doing in my kitchen? And how did you get in here?" I screamed, totally freaked out that he was standing in my kitchen.

"I followed you home last night because I was concerned about how you were feeling. You left your door unlocked, so I let myself in after your friends pulled off." He turned towards the stove wearing my dad's favorite barb-a-cue apron.

Okay, for just a second, I felt like I'd met a stalker. I couldn't believe this man was standing in my kitchen cooking. He could have harmed me last night, but the fact that he didn't made me feel a little at ease. I thought about how I would get him out of my house before my parents came home.

"Look, Malik, this was very nice of you, but my parents will be home this morning. I don't think they'll be too happy to see a strange man standing in their kitchen."

"A grown woman can't have company?" he asked, a little surprised.

I fought with myself as to whether or not this was a good time to tell him my real age. He wouldn't be interested anymore if he knew that I was only seventeen. Malik looked at my blank stare, grabbed my hands and pulled me close to him. I wrapped my arms around his waist and exhaled. He rubbed his nose against mine. I thought that was so sweet. I felt loved.

"Look, baby girl, I'll go before your parents get home." He kissed me and sat me down at the table. "But before I go, just appreciate and enjoy the breakfast I made." I sat like a good girl and ate every morsel. I couldn't believe how well he cooked.

Around ten minutes after nine, I heard a car pull up in the driveway. My heart pounded. I dropped my fork and ran to the door. An unfamiliar gray Mercedes sat in front of my house. *Who could that be?* A very distinguished Spanish man in a black suit was headed towards my door. I opened it before he had a chance to ring the bell.

"May I help you, sir?"

"Yes, I'm looking for a Malik Johnson," he said, in a Cuban accent.

Confused, I stepped back. "Malik?" I said. "He doesn't live here."

"I know, ma'am, but I know he's here now."

I asked the man to wait right there. I jetted to get Malik. This one was definitely the straw that broke the camel's back. I stormed towards the kitchen, knocking over my mother's favorite Italian vase, only to find no Malik.

"Malik, stop playing!" I yelled, in frustration. "Malik, Malik!" There was no answer.

As I turned around to let the man know Malik had disappeared, he was standing in the kitchen doorway.

Excuse me, sir, I asked that you wait at the front door," I said, with an attitude.

"I'm sorry, ma'am, but I heard you calling his name and figured he would try and run."

"Look, I don't know what's going on, but I don't know Malik that well. I don't know what kind of business he's into, but I want no parts of it." The man looked at me very strangely, almost as if to suggest that I was lying.

"Well, ma'am, when you see Mr. Johnson again, tell him to contact Mr. Riley Escobar." He handed me his business card. "And let him know that he can run, but he can't hide. Tell him I'm on his tracks every step of the way. He knows exactly what I mean. I must caution you, be very careful in dealing with this guy, he's bad news."

What did he mean by that? I let Mr. Escobar out, unsure of what to say. As soon as I closed the door behind him, I ran to the phone to call Denim. By the third ring, I became frantic. I tapped my foot hoping someone would answer. On the fifth ring, Ms. Douglas answered.

"Good morning," she said, in her usual pleasant tone. Denim's mom was the total opposite of her. She was a very sweet, holy woman. Denim was more like her father and his side of the family.

"Hi, Ms. Douglas, is Denim awake?" I struggled to use my most normal voice.

"No, Niyah, but I'll get her lazy butt up if you want me to."

I laughed, because she was right, Denim would sleep all day if you let her. "That's okay, just have her call me when she comes to."

"Not a problem, sweetheart."

Seconds later, I heard keys jingling at the door. That was usually the way my parents let me know that they were entering the house. I tried to clean the dishes off the table as quickly as possible. No questions, no problems. I blew out the candle and waited by the door to surprise them. As soon as my dad placed his foot on the wood tile, I jumped on him like a baby chimp in the wild.

"How's my princess?" he said, as he swung me around.

"Fine daddy! Where's mom?" Before he could answer, I saw her lugging her bags up the steps. "Hey, mom!"

"Hi, baby." Her island tan was beautiful.

"Boy, you guys look well rested," I helped her with her bags. I was so thrilled for them to be home.

"I see the house is clean," my mom said.

"I hope you didn't have any wild parties," my dad smirked as he picked up mom's Italian vase from the floor.

I had forgotten just that quickly about her vase, and that psychotic Malik. I didn't have a clue where that fool had gone. I just prayed he wasn't hiding under my dad's bed. I was still uneasy about Mr. Escobar. *Who was he really?* The phone rang in the middle of my thought.

I heard my dad say, "Excuse me, who is this?" My anxiety got the best of me, so I ran to the phone. "This man on the phone says he wants to talk to you." He held the phone away from his ear.

"Uuh, who did he say he was?" I asked, with a stutter.

"Ma-lick," he said, handing me the phone.

With the bat of my eyes, I gently took the phone from him. He gave me the, *we need to talk when you're finished* look. I smiled and spoke into the phone.

"Hello."

"Yeah, baby girl, what's up? I guess I left just in time, huh?"

I tried to sound as normal as possible. "Yeah. Where are you?"

"Yo, I had to slip out your basement door and chill until dude left. I slid around the front and, as I eased in my car, I saw the cab drop your peeps off. Yo, your mom is fine."

"Uh, excuse me."

"Anyway, that's why I had to jet."

"Well, who was that man?" He paused.

"I'll get into that later. How about dinner tonight?"

"I don't know, I'll page you later." I walked over to the sink to fill the dishwasher. "Hello," I said. There was a long silence on the other end.

"I'll check you later," he said and hung up the phone.

I guess he didn't like my answer. I stared at the phone with the ugliest face I could find. I couldn't believe his actions.

Later on that day, my mom and I sat and talked about my weekend. I told her that Denim and I had gone to the movies to see '*Baby Boy.*' She knew that we had found time to hang out at the mall, because that's what we did in our spare time. She got part truth and part lie about Malik. I told her I had met him at the Cheltenham Mall. I lied about his age and his work status. To tell the truth, I didn't know at that point if he even had a job. She warned me to watch myself, because all boys my age wanted to do was make babies. That was the same speech I got every time I met a new guy.

Now, my dad didn't like boys too much. He said that he was their age once and knew how their minds worked. "They didn't," he would say. "The only thing that worked on them is their hands and you know what else," he'd preach. I used to get so embarrassed. But what parents fail to realize is that when they repeat the same thing fifty times, teens tune them out after the fifth time.

This one guy I dated, I thought my dad was going to make

his life short. He was one of the hip-hop types. Entering my house with his pants hanging down, speaking nothing but Ebonics was not Mr. Christian's idea of a good candidate for his daughter. My father prided himself on his old school gentleman-like manners. To top it off, Keith's phone manners were limited to, "Yo, what up, Niyah there?" My dad would cringe. I had to get rid of Keith quick because I got no peace befriending him. Keith was definitely a nobody.

My concentration was broken when I heard my dad say, "Hey, Denim, how are you?"

* * *

It was four o'clock in the afternoon and this chick was just getting out. "What's up Ms. J-Ho," Denim said, as she plopped in my dad's chair.

"Why I gotta be J-Ho," I said, pushing her feet off of my mother's coffee table.

"You were all hemmed up last night. That jerk wouldn't let you come up for air."

"Don't be jealous, girl." I motioned for her to go upstairs to my room.

It took me forty minutes to give her the details from the previous night events. She kept interrupting me with questions. Denim didn't look too happy about me kissing Malik on the first day. She said he could have had Mono or something. When I told her about that morning in the kitchen, she really flipped. As crazy as she acted, I knew that I couldn't tell her too much after that.

"So, what's up? Are you going to make him your man or what?" Denim asked, after I had finished.

"I don't know, it's a possibility."

"Well, I got to run some errands for my mom. What are you

gettin' into later?"

"I got a date tonight." Denim sucked her teeth and switched out of my bedroom. The green on her face proved envy. I understood. Me having a man broke our normal routine.

* * *

At nine o'clock sharp the doorbell rang. I ran to get it, but my dad beat me to it.

"Yes, sir, may I help you?" I heard my dad say.

"My name is Malik Johnson and I'm here to pick up Niyah."

I froze in the middle of the stairs. My heart fell into the pit of my stomach. I had told Malik that I would meet him at the 7-11, so why was he at my door. I'm sure he sat in the front of the class because he definitely wasn't a good listener.

I tried to play it off. "Hey, Malik," I said, moving closer to my dad. "Dad, this is Malik, Malik, this is my dad, Mr. Christian."

"Niyah, we've already met." My father's tone grew stern.

I was shocked because Malik held two half dozen roses in his hands for my mother and me. He even purchased cigars for my dad. He must have seen his cigar case when he snuck in my house the night before. Neither of my parents were impressed.

"Niyah, may I speak to you?" my dad said. He strolled towards the kitchen.

Oh boy, I thought, *this is gonna get serious*. I followed in my parent's direction. "Not another tag team," I huffed.

"This won't be long since your company is waiting," my dad said.

As soon as we got in the kitchen, my mother jumped right in. "How much do you know about this young man?" she asked. "He seems nice, but he looks and sounds much too old for you."

Her questions shot at me like bullets.

I had to think of a good lie. "Um, he's nineteen." My dad looked at me unimpressed.

"Where are you two going tonight?" my mom asked. I expected more questioning from my father.

"We're going to the movies and I promise to be home by twelve."

"Not a minute later," my dad finally spoke. He kissed me on the cheek then left out the kitchen.

I snatched my purse and headed out the door with my new boo. Malik opened the car door for me and I slid in his SUV like Cinderella. He took me all around Philly. I saw places I never knew existed. I didn't expect him to buy me anything, but he did. I was now the proud new owner of a black Prada bag. I knew I would be the envy of the girls in my neighborhood. They didn't care much for Denim or me anyway.

Malik was so gentle with me. He held my hand whenever we walked through the streets. And he fed me shrimp at Red Lobster. I felt like a queen. I vowed to only date older men after that night.

We cruised up to my door at 11:45 pm. I could see my parents' television light on in their bedroom. My dad loved to watch the old sitcoms on Nick@Nite. Reruns of *The Jefferson's* were his favorite.

As I unsnapped my seatbelt, Malik stroked my hand. "I hope you enjoyed yourself tonight, Ma." He kissed me gently on my lips. That was one of a million. Counting every one, I guess put me in the pressed section of the class.

"The most wonderful time ever," I said, as I kissed him back.

"I'ma pick you up tomorrow at three, so be ready." I loved the way he took charge.

Without thinking about the next day plans, I agreed and

jumped out of the car. As I headed for the door, I fumbled in my purse for my keys. The door swung open as I pulled them out.

"Oh, hey Dad!" I said, as I pranced past him. He gave me a curious look.

"I'm glad to see you're home on time. Did you and that young man have fun?"

I let my smile serve as my answer and skipped upstairs to my bedroom. I was certainly on cloud nine. I was slipping into my pajamas when my phone rang. I picked up the receiver in fear.

"Hello," I whispered.

"Hey, baby. I just wanted to make sure you got in safely. And I wanted to tell you that I love you."

My heart went pitter-patter. I couldn't believe he cared that much. How many guys would call to make sure I was fine right after dropping me off. And when he told me he loved me, I could have died. I let him know that I loved him too and that I'd see him the next day.

In my sleep, I could hear my phone ringing. Wearily, I let it ring, but the person on the other end was relentless. The clock read 9:00 am. I stuck my head under the pillow to block out the sound, but that didn't stop the annoying noise. Finally, I reached from under the cover, wrestling to grab the receiver. In my attempt, I hit the speaker button instead.

I couldn't believe that it was Malik on the other end speaking sweet nothings in my ear. I was irritated, but decided not to crush his ego. In the middle of listening to how much he'd missed me, my other line beeped. I asked him to hold on, but he didn't seem too pleased that he was being made to wait.

"Well, well, well," I heard Denim's voice say through the speaker.

"Hey, girl, what's up?" I didn't know why she was up so early.

"The question isn't what's up with me. What's up with you?"

"Nothing girl. I'm talking to Malik on the other line, can I call you back?" I said, still groggy.

I could hear the disappointment in Denim's reply. "Remember this is our day for the mall. Call me right back so we can set up a time to meet. I was thinking around three would be good."

Dang, I had forgotten all about our shopping day. I didn't want to upset her, so I told her that I'd call her right back. When I clicked back over to Malik, I heard him having a conversation with a female in the background.

"Yeah, I want jelly on my toast," I heard him say. "Hello," he said, turning his attention back to me once he heard me click back over.

"Yeah, I'm here," I said. "Who's that?"

"Oh, umm, that's my cousin, Nicole. She's in town for the weekend." I didn't know much about his family, so I had no reason not to believe him. "Now, back to us," he said.

"Well, some things have changed. I promised Denim that I'd go with her to the mall today. Can we postpone our date for later on this evening?" Once again he expressed his disappointment by saying not a word.

"Look, I didn't go through all of this trouble planning a surprise picnic today just for you to cancel on me!" he shouted.

"Oh, I'm sorry," I said, with a tear in my eye. I thought it was so sweet of him to go through all that trouble to organize a picnic just for me. How in the world could I let him down?

"Okay," I said, "I'll work it out. Pick me up at three."

"Baby, that's why I love you," he said.

Needless to say, I cancelled my plans with Denim. She was pissed, but I thought, *mall or man,* and I had to go with the man. He would be the biggest pay off for me in the end.

Teenage Bluez

*   *   *

Weeks went by and I hadn't heard from or seen Denim. My relationship with Malik was getting more and more serious. My parents were having a fit that I was spending all my time with him.

"You have to be careful," my mother said one morning, while at breakfast.

"Look, Mom, you've already told me about the birds and the bees. Besides, Malik isn't like that, he hasn't disrespected me in any way."

"He better not," my father eased in. "I'll kill him if he does!"

All the pressure I felt from my family and Denim for dating Malik only pushed me closer to him. I knew he loved me because he bought me so many things and he always wanted to spend time with me. Deep down inside I wished I could have it all. Why couldn't I have my man and my best friend too? Denim not returning my calls disturbed me.

I got up from the table to get dressed because Malik was picking me up in an hour. We were going to Atlantic City. I took extra care to look really sexy. I didn't want any bathing suit babes getting my man's attention. I sported my pink cotton, tightly fitted capri's and a pretty light pink, blue and white striped strapless halter. I swept my hair up into a neat ponytail. Spiral strands of hair dangled lightly around the edges.

Malik's smile spelled satisfaction. "Darn, baby girl, I'm gonna have to keep you locked up lookin' like that."

I blushed as I closed the door. I reclined the passenger seat and rolled up the black tinted window. Malik turned up the music and we cruised off in his new Hummer.

It didn't matter that I wasn't old enough; I gambled like a pro. I won seventy-five dollars on the quarter slot machine. We hit every casino on the strip. Malik always kept plenty of money in his pockets, so anything I wanted I got. It was strange how he could never tell me what kind of job he had. He said that all I had to do was worry about being pretty and keeping him happy.

By the time we finished eating at an All-U-Can-Eat seafood buffet, it was twelve o'clock in the morning. I knew my parents would be upset, because twelve was the time I should've been walking through the door. We were still forty-five minutes away in driving distance.

"Niyah, I was thinking maybe we can get a room at the Trump Towers," Malik said.

I almost choked on my champagne. My eyes grew big. I knew deep down inside that it would eventually come to this. What man would keep spending his money and not expect to receive something in return?

"Well, I don't know," I said trembling. "I don't want to rush things."

Malik pushed his chair away from the table with squinted eyebrows. "All this money I'm spending on you; the trips, the fine dinners, the high dollar bags, and this is the thanks I get."

His voice sent chills down my spine. I was too afraid to look him in the face. *How can I get out of this,* I thought. I had never slept with a boy before, let alone a man.

"Can we just go home and make plans to spend the night together another time?" I asked.

Malik slammed his fist down on the table. Thank God there were only two other couples in the restaurant because I was so embarrassed. He dug in his pocket and threw a fifty-dollar bill at me. He stormed out of the restaurant. I felt so bad for making him angry. I thought about what my parents would say if I didn't come home. *What was the most they could do to me,* I thought. They had stopped giving me spankings a long time ago, so they wouldn't do that. The most they could do was ground me for a month. I decided to test the waters and stay out with him anyway. After all, I did love him and he loved me.

I slowly got up from the table and headed for the door. When I reached the boardwalk, I saw Malik sitting on the bench lighting a cigarette. He saw me coming towards him and walked away.

"Wait!" I yelled, as I ran to catch up to him. The night air pushed me back with every move. He stopped when he reached the only 24-hour convenience store.

Crying uncontrollably, I agreed to stay. He gently hugged me and told me that he was sorry for yelling at me in the restaurant. Malik led me into the store. I saw a few t-shirts I wanted and threw them in a basket. I attempted to pay for my items, but he made me put away my money.

"My woman never has to pay for anything, not even a pack of gum," he said. The fat, white bald man behind the counter smiled in admiration. I could tell he was surprised to see a young black couple so in love.

"What did you buy?" I asked.

"Oh, something for you." He kept walking.

* * *

There I was lying in a fancy suite at the Trump Towers. The red velvet comforter felt good against my skin. I flipped through the channels on the plasma television and stopped on *'That's So Raven.'* I loved Raven Simone. I rolled over on the bed and noticed a familiar card sticking out of Malik's pants pocket. I heard the shower and figured I had time to play detective.

Easing over to his jeans, I pulled the card all the way out. It read, "Riley Escobar, counselor/director of Hibachi." *That's the guy who showed up at my house last Sunday morning. What in the world is Hibachi?* Counselor? Is he crazy? Am I dealing with a lunatic?

I heard Malik coming and stuffed the card back in his pocket. He came out of the bathroom with just his towel wrapped around his waist. I got really scared. Butterflies fluttered around in my stomach. He came over to me and removed my sandals.

"Get comfortable, baby. It's gonna be a long night," he said, massaging my feet.

What did he mean by that? I didn't know what to say or do. He told me to go into the bathroom and take a shower. When I closed the bathroom door, I saw a beautiful Victoria's Secret pink nightgown waiting for me behind the door. I had a difficult time turning on the shower.

"Niyah, what's taking you so long?" Malik yelled from the bedroom. I was afraid to tell him that I didn't know how to turn on the water, but I had no choice.

"I can't seem to work the shower," I said.

He walked through the door, picked up a remote and pointed it towards the shower sensor. "You regulate the temperature with this button," he said, slapping me on my butt. I jumped and almost fell in the shower.

As the large suds from the body wash formed on my legs, I felt a cool breeze come in over the shower door.

"Malik?" I asked.

"Yeah, it's me. Can I join you?" I was so scared.

Oh no, I thought. The only person who had seen me even halfway naked at this age was Denim.

"Sure," I said, tensely.

Malik had a way of putting me at ease. He washed my back very softly and, as he began to massage my shoulders, I began to relax even more. All the steam in the bathroom made me drowsy. He turned off the water and stepped out of the shower to reach for the towel. I hadn't been dried off since I was in the cradle. He applied lotion to my body with Victoria's Secret, '*Very Sexy Lotion for Her.*' Malik sprinkled the same brand of glittering powder on my neck and back. I was shining like new money.

Dressed in my Vicky's gown, he led me to the bed that was laced with white satin sheets. The way he laid me down, he made me forget all about my morals, my principles, and my parents. Despite my promise to Denim, I was willing to go all the way. I never considered the dangers.

Malik rested his head in my neck. "You smell so good," he whined, as he sniffed harder. "Close your eyes and relax. Trust me," he said. He rubbed every inch of my body.

I did just what he said. I shut the world out of my mind. My body was his playground. He slowly removed my nightgown. I couldn't understand why he didn't want to cut off the lights, but at that point, it didn't matter. I was prepared to give him all of me.

After kissing me everywhere, I felt the big move coming. I braced myself, unsure of what to expect. I remember Denim telling me that if I ever got in a situation where I had to do *it*, then I should always protect myself. I even thought back to the pep talks from various counselors at the school. They always discussed the fact that abstinence is the best form of birth control, but use a condom when I put myself in a stupid situation. Although my mind raced, I managed to say something.

I tapped Malik on his shoulder and said, "Do you have a condom?"

He moaned like a baby. "Just let me feel you for a minute, then I'll get it," he said.

As he pressed more and more, I became uneasy. "Get it," I said, as I inched back. Frustrated, he went to remove the condom from his pants pocket.

Seconds later, I was experiencing the most painful feeling I'd ever felt in my life. Malik was enjoying himself, but I was suffering. I pretended to be happy just to please him. Soon, Malik was done. To my surprise, he told me the condom had broken!

"Oh, my God!" I screamed. "Where's the condom?"

Malik stood in front of me, calm and cool. "Baby, don't worry, I got out just in time."

I shifted the covers over my naked body. "Are you sure?" I asked.

He shook his head with confidence. Malik crawled back into bed and hugged me tightly. We fell asleep until checkout at twelve the next afternoon.

Malik dropped me off like I was a stranger. Before my feet hit the pavement, he was three blocks away. I had no time to focus my attention on him. I was sure my parents were waiting for me.

As I turned the key, I felt the tension at the door. My mom was sitting on the steps still in her nightclothes, with big bags underneath her eyes. When I closed the door, I felt a slap to the back of my head. I quickly turned only to see my dad's beet red face.

"Where in the hell have you been?" he screamed, preparing to hit me again. I ducked to avoid the next attack.

"Let me explain," I cried.

"Young lady, you better make it good," my mother growled.

"Me and Malik broke down coming back from Atlantic City."

"Atlantic City!" my dad yelled. "You're not old enough to gamble!"

"Are you having sex with this boy?" my mom threw in.

"No, can I please go on with my story?" My mother ran her

fingers through her hair as she stared at my dad. There was a moment of silence and I went on.

"We were stuck in darkness on the side of the road and had no way of contacting anyone. No one stopped to help us, and neither one of our cell phones were charged."

"I can't believe that no one stopped to help two kids on the side of a dark road," my dad griped.

I never expected my parents to be that upset. And my dad hitting me was even more devastating. They told me I was grounded for six months. My room and cell phone privileges were revoked. My dad threatened that if Malik called or came to the house, he would kill him. There was no way I could call to warn him.

*   *   *

Weeks passed and I began to feel really sick. My clothes grew smaller and, to top it off, sleep wouldn't leave me alone. I waited for my monthly friend, but she never showed. I knew deep down that I was pregnant. Nevertheless, I blamed it on stress, and went on with my daily routines.

On September 18th, I sat in Chemistry class two rows behind Denim. We hadn't spoken since the summer and, once school started, people knew we were no longer friends. Because I had abandoned everyone in my life, I was lonely. My parents said very little to me. I felt like a prisoner in my own home. I hadn't heard from Malik since our night at Trump Towers. He hadn't even tried to contact me. I would check my cell phone messages from school, no Malik.

The bell rang and all the students rushed out at once.

"Denim, can I please talk to you?" I asked her, once we were in the hall.

She kept walking as if I said nothing. A few of our once

enemies snickered when they saw what she did. I needed her so bad at that time, if she only knew how sad I was. I walked towards the cafeteria with my head hung low. People pushed and shoved me as if I didn't exist.

It was hard for me to see Denim with other girls. I yearned to have my friend back. She started hanging out with Missi, Anita and Yolanda, the popular girls from the cheerleading team. We despised them last year. They were very stuck up.

I entered the lunchroom and saw the three of them at the table with some other girls from the squad. Yolanda looked at me and sucked her teeth. That didn't bother me, seeing Denim laughing with them did.

"You lookin' busted to me, girl," Missi said, looking me up and down.

My confidence was shot. My lips felt permanently sealed. I decided against lunch and walked out. I ran to the bathroom on the eighth floor, which was always empty. I dropped my books on the floor and ran into the stall. Before I could put my face in the toilet, I threw up all over the tiles. Everything was a blur.

A very quiet unpopular girl came in and asked if I needed help. I told her no, I was fine. She used the bathroom and walked out. I ended up missing my gym class because it took me about a half hour to get it together.

That night I cried myself to sleep. I wished I could close my eyes and never wake up again. Nothing mattered to me anymore. I felt like my whole life was ruined and all because of a man. Dealing with Malik seemed good at first, but it came with a big price tag.

The next day as I got ready for school, I could hear my parents talking.

"Don't you think we can let her off punishment?" my mom asked.

"No, she's got to learn the hard way," my dad replied.

Teenage Bluez

I dragged myself downstairs feeling tired. "Good morning." They looked at me and didn't say two words. I picked my books up off the sofa table.

My mom must have felt bad. She wished me a good day as I opened the door. I turned hoping my dad would speak. He shot me his usual disgusted frown.

As I headed towards school, I decided not to go. I figured it was best for me to take a trip to the mall to sort out my problems. I tossed my notebooks in the trash and hopped on the bus. I decided to visit the King of Prussia mall. No one would stop me there. *Denim and I had been there during school hours before.*

My first stop was Nordstroms. It brought back memories of Malik on one of our many shopping sprees. I had to get out of there. I went in a few more stores just to look around. As I came out of Macy's, I began to feel dizzy. I sat down on the bench. After a few minutes, I experienced a sense of relief. I got up and before I knew it, I had passed out. And that's how I made it to the hospital.

* * *

When I turned my head, I saw Denim coming through the door. She ran to the bed in awe.

"How did you know I was here?" I asked. Denim just hugged me like Nettie did Celie in *'The Color Purple.'* I knew then that God did answer prayers.

The doctor came in behind the nurse. They both looked concerned.

"Ma'am, I'm going to have to ask you to step out of the room," the tall dark-skinned doctor said to Denim.

"Please let her stay," I begged. "Whatever you have to say to me, you can say it in front of her." He gave me a strange glance.

"Are you sure?"

"Sure as my test results," I said.

"Okay, Ms. Christian. We administered a pregnancy test and it was positive."

Denim looked at me in shame. "Oh, Niyah, tell me you didn't."

I covered my face with my hands. Denim began to cry like she was the one pregnant.

"Also," he went on, "it's routine for us to test for all venereal diseases once we discover a woman to be pregnant."

A huge lump formed in my throat. *What is he saying?* Denim stared at me as if she were going to pass out.

"Your HIV test results were positive as well."

Denim hit the floor. She blacked out on the spot. All attention went to her. The nurse raced to her side to resuscitate her. I was so numb I couldn't react. I laid there motionless. *What will my parents think? I totally screwed up my life. One bad choice caused me to hurt, not only my best friend and family but, most of all, myself. He told me to trust him and I did. Now look where it's gotten me. Lord, if You're real, help me.*

*　*　*

"Oh, Jesus, I thought I told you to be careful!" my mom cried uncontrollably when I gave her and my dad part of the bad news. Denim had come home with me from the hospital and was right there by my side the entire time.

"That's only part of what I have to tell you," I said, afraid.

My dad paced so hard he wore out the carpet. Because he never got over the fact that I stayed out all night, he lost it. His lack of words confirmed he would snap. Denim stood like a statue. I could tell she wanted no parts of this. It's rare that she has nothing to say, but that day she couldn't be paid to speak.

"What do you mean that's not the entire story?" my Mom barely got out. She took short heavy breaths.

For some reason, I couldn't get the second part out. I looked at Denim for support. "Well, Mrs. Christian…."

"Shut up, Denim! This is Niyah's mess, so let her speak!" My dad walked closer towards me. By this time, everyone was crying but him.

"They tested me for HIV and it came back positive," I said.

My dad punched a hole through the wall. My mother fell off the couch, hitting her head on the edge of the coffee table. When my dad saw blood, he cracked.

"You whore!" he screamed. "Look what you've done to our family!" He picked my mother up from the floor to check her head.

"Mom!" I cried, running to her side.

"Get your hands off of my wife!" He pushed me into the wall. Demin ran out of the house, she couldn't take it anymore.

My dad told me to get my things and get out of his house. Claiming that no daughter of his was that stupid to get pregnant and catch some nasty disease, he made me feel lower than dirt.

"Where am I supposed to go?" I hollered.

"You figure it out," he said. "Just know that here is not where you belong."

I gathered as many things as I could and headed out the door to nowhere. In the midst of my packing, I came across Mr. Escobar's business card. Since Malik had changed his cell phone number, I was going to get answers from Mr. Escobar. I walked the streets for hours before getting up the nerve to call.

"Mr. Escobar speaking."

"Hi, my name is Niyah Christian and you gave me your card one day while looking for Malik." He told me to refresh his memory because he had many young women he'd met in regards to Malik. I felt sick.

"You came to my house on Stenton Avenue and Vernon Road."

"Oh yes. Have you found Mr. Johnson?" The sound of Malik's name caused me to burst into tears.

"No, I haven't seen Malik in weeks. He's even changed his cell phone number. I was calling, hoping that you could tell me how to get in touch with him."

Come to find out, Mr. Escobar was an AIDS counselor. He said that Malik had been on a rampage infecting young women in the Philadelphia area. Malik treated all of his victims very well, and then convinced them to sleep with him. Mr. Escobar admitted that he pretended to use condoms, but always seems to poke holes in them. He then left his victims with no way to contact him, pretty much how he did me.

When Malik first discovered he was infected, he would speak with Mr. Escobar on a regular basis. For some reason, he snapped and stopped showing up to his counseling sessions. Mr. Escobar began receiving reports from Malik's wife, Nicole, that she had proof he was infecting others out of anger. She was infected by him and found no need to leave. Who would want her? She let him run the streets, but reported him when she found out that he was infecting young girls my age. Yes, just when I couldn't be more hurt, I discovered he was married.

Mr. Escobar said that Malik was dangerous and on the run. That's why he was looking for him the day he showed up at my house. I asked him why he didn't tell me. He said that it was unconstitutional to tell Malik's business even though his actions were at the expense of others. That was homicidal in my mind. Mr. Escobar did express that if he were caught, he would be imprisoned for life. I explained to him that I was pregnant, infected and homeless. He invited me to meet him at his office for assistance.

He registered me into "Safe Haven," a shelter for teens in

my situation. I didn't like it but it was better than being on the street.

For several weeks, I tried to call home, but my father would hang up on me every time. I talked to Denim every day. She was having a very hard time handling my situation. She told me that she had been talking to my mother regularly. She wanted to see me, but was too afraid to consult my dad because he was still in such a rage.

My days seemed long at "Safe Haven," but at least I was getting the counseling and medical support I needed. There were days when I felt like just ending it all. I never went to church or even knew about God. I was a pro at calling on some man in the sky in my time of trouble.

This situation has brought me to a deeper relationship with God. We have church service every Sunday at the shelter and I've learned a lot about faith and walking by it. My baby is kicking and even though I have not finished school, I'm proud to say that I'll be a mother in just a few weeks. God forgives our sins, but in order for us to learn, something has to die. And that something that died on the day that I gave my virginity to Malik was possibly my life, the life of my unborn child and the loss of my relationship with my parents and my best friend. I had to ask myself, was one night of sex worth all that I lost?

UNBROKEN PROMISES
by Kwiecia Cain

"Oh shoot, I'm late again!" were the words that flew out of my mouth after hearing the third period late bell ring. Trying to make it to class before my pressed English teacher, Ms. Caldwell, slams her door and sends me to the principal's office for tardiness is always an issue. Hearing Ms. Caldwell say, "Kourtney Taylor, you're late!" drives me crazy. Born in Brooklyn, New York and raised in Washington, D.C., I'm used to hearing people scream, but she takes it to the next level.

Now, I know you've heard that Brooklyn females don't take nothing from nobody, which is true. But when people hear that you used to live in Brooklyn and now live in DC, you know what you get? *Plain old haters.* In my mind a hater is defined as one who envies you because of the talents God has blessed you with. Well, unfortunately for me, I'm envied by almost everyone at Jesse Ward High School. Because of that jealousy, my sophomore year has been nothing but drama.

It all started at the pep rally that my school held at the beginning of the basketball season. This year I was elected as captain of the cheerleading squad and my boyfriend, Rashard Brooks, was elected captain of the basketball team. Some people can't seem to appreciate our talents and share in the happiness; especially Stefanie Banks. Stef wanted to be captain so bad that I think she was willing to kill for it.

Teenage Bluez

I never understood why she would hate on me for being named captain when she knows I'm the best person for the job. I'm not the type to toot my own horn, but I know that I have what it takes to lead my squad to the championship. I'm not saying I'm better than everyone, but I know I have more skills than most of the girls on my team. The fact that I've been cheering since I was three years old for the Force Spirit All-Stars National Cheerleading Squad, whom I still cheer for, had a lot to do with it. At age 16, I had 13 years of pure cheering under my belt.

Most people don't realize how much hard work goes into being a Force Spirit cheerleader. Traveling around the country to compete in different competitions for various awards can be grueling for a girl my age. However, I've always been up for the challenge. Anyway, since a lot of people don't know the complexity of the sport, they constantly continue to discourage me; everyone except my mother Terry Green.

Even though she can be nerve wrecking, Terry is like a sister to me. She even lets me call her Terri from time to time. Although a young mother, she understands my pain, is my number one fan, and my worst critic. My mother and I share the same love for cheerleading. She's the cheerleading coach for the younger squad of the Force Spirit. In fact, she was my coach until last year. When we're at home, she still coaches and pushes me when I need that extra push, or when I lose my focus. She truly believes that cheering is my destiny. Because of that, she's never missed any of my competitions.

Because my mother is a coach, she knows when I mess up; and she has no problem letting me know what I did wrong and how I can avoid doing it the next time. Her encouragement and promises to target cheer scouts for me this year keeps me going. We both know that a scholarship would be my ticket to college.

My parents, who had been married for 10 years, divorced

right after I was born. After the divorce, my father, Charles Taylor, moved from Brooklyn to Manhattan, a couple blocks from Wall Street so he'd be near his newly acquired front office job. My mom and I stayed in Brooklyn until I was about two years old, at which time she decided to move to Washington, DC. for better job opportunities. It's been rough for her raising me all alone. But she's doing a heck of a job.

*   *   *

After rushing and finally heading toward my English class, the unthinkable happened. I ran into Rashard, my one and only love, which I don't usually see until after school. I've been in love with Rashard since I was in the ninth grade. But, at that time, he wouldn't give me the time of day. Rashard has a reputation for only dating popular chicks. If you're voted best dressed, got the fanciest car in the school, or the best cheerleader in the school; then you might have a chance at Rashard. *Otherwise, forget about it.* He always says, "His woman has to make him look good."

Rashard and I got together almost a year ago. As the news traveled through the school, the haters went wild, especially Stef. She couldn't believe Rashard would date a sophomore when he's a senior. She wanted him bad! On top of that, she cheers with me, so I've been flaunting our relationship in her face since day one.

I was surprised to see Rashard in the hallway. He was as fine as they come now days; real dark like milk chocolate. Immediately his dark brown eyes began to mesmerize me as he kissed me. I just went with the flow, not knowing what I was doing. He gently guided me with his tongue for several hot seconds. All of a sudden, visions of my mom walking up behind me and snatching me by the collar of my shirt had me paranoid. I quickly pulled away from Rashard's magnetic lips. I ended our little incident by telling him to meet me at my locker after school and quickly hurried to class.

When I arrived at my English class, I discovered we had a substitute who really didn't care whether I was late or not. She just told me to come in, take a worksheet and sit down. I followed her instructions, but the whole 90 minutes I sat in class thinking about Rashard's 5'10 physique brushing up against my body. I started to feel mushy inside as if I were falling in love with him. I didn't know what brought this feeling on. I remembered having reservations about getting into a relationship with a 12th grader considering I was only a sophomore. Besides our age difference, I wasn't sure how my mom would feel about his long dreads, which were kinda like my dad's.

The ringing of the bell snapped me back into reality. After class, I caught up with my girl, Jontice, and as we were walking to lunch, I began telling her about my kiss with Rashard in the hallway. She told me it was sweet and began to describe how she felt when she experienced her first kiss. That was just like Jontice, always putting the attention on herself.

Once we got our lunch, we sat down at the table with Bre and Maleka. They started talking about our math test next period, but I really wasn't paying attention because I was thinking about Rashard and the kiss we had shared. I could still feel his lips on mine.

After lunch, Jontice, Bre, Maleka and I began to walk to our fourth period class. We all had one thing in common, cheering was a priority for everyone in our clique, and we all cheered for Force Spirit.

"Dang, we got another sub. At this rate, we're never gonna learn anything," Jontice said, as we walked into our math class.

"Well, look on the bright side. At least we don't have to

worry about taking that test," I said.

"That's cool. But Ms. Kourtney, did something happen to you earlier that you want to share with us?" Maleka stated, as we were taking our seats.

"What makes you think something happened to me today?" I quizzed.

"Well, because during lunch you had this glow on your face, and Jontice told us to ask you about what happened to you on your way to third period." Maleka looked extremely serious.

Maleka was the one in our crew who every time you looked around, had a different boyfriend. These days she was stuck on Lennert Simmons. He was in the 12th grade too. He and Rashard are jive close in friendship, but Lennert is all about football. *No girls, no parties, just football.*

Maleka had been named co-captain of our school's cheerleading squad and she had the skill of flipping down pat. Now, I'm not gonna front, Maleka was just as good as me in cheering and that's why I knew with her as co-captain, our team was gonna be number one. *Stef was good too, but you'd have to shoot me to admit it.*

"Okay," I finally said, getting frustrated at the fact that she was rushing me. "I was getting my books for English out of my locker when the late bell rang. I was rushing to get to class when I ran into Rashard. He called me over and began to slobber me down right there in the hallway. I became embarrassed, but told him to meet me at my locker after school."

"Well, now that's what I call true love," Bre said, dramatically flinging her hand on her forehead. She was the drama queen out of the whole clique. She's about 5'5, with a light brown complexion and flawless skin. All she ever talked about was finding her true love.

"Love!" Jontice said. "Bre, please spare me the ignorance."

Teenage Bluez

* * *

It was 3:15 and the last bell rang at 3:30. I could hardly wait to get to my locker to see Rashard. At the sound of the last bell of the day, I picked my books up and zoomed out of class. I met up with Maleka and, when we got to my locker Rashard was nowhere to be found.

"Hey baby," a young male voice said from behind. My hopes began to rise, but when I turned around, I found out it was only Lennert.

"What's up? Where you been all day? I missed you," Maleka said, with a dramatic sound to her voice. *She fell for guys too easily*.

"What's up, Kourtney? Heard about your lovemaking on the Green Floor earlier," Lennert said, laughing.

I was ready to slap him silly when Rashard walked up and brought the sun with him. Rashard and I kissed immediately for about five minutes. Then, he decided he would drive me home. Rashard had a silver Impala with very dark tinted windows and a sound system that was tight. It had a ten CD changer and a DVD that played movies on a TV that sat up on the dashboard. I loved riding in his car. His parents had bought it for him for his senior year. He got good grades, was an outstanding basketball player; and they were wealthy. Obviously, they weren't worried about him getting a basketball scholarship. Me on the other hand, I'd have to work for mine.

The ride to my house was silent until Rashard broke it up with the unthinkable question. "Baby, how do you feel about me?"

My mind raced. I tried to think of a quick answer. "Well, let's just say you're very special to me." I thought that was a good answer.

"No baby, do you love me?" he asked.

"I got love for you. If something was to happen to you I'd be sad," I said, unable to tell Rashard what he wanted to hear.

"Baby, we've been together almost a year and you still can't say you love me. Look, Kourtney, I'm in love with you and anything you need or want, know that Rashard Terrence Brooks will try to provide it for you. I put that on everything I love," he said, with a very sincere look on his face. Besides the whole school loves you.

"Is that why you love me?" I had a really strange look on my face. "Would you love me if I weren't well known?"

"Of course. I'll call you later," he said, deciding to drop the subject for now. He poked his lips out for a kiss.

"A'ight," I said. I jumped out of the car.

"You just gonna leave me hanging?" he asked, when I opened the car door.

After giving him a quick kiss, I ran into the house to call my girl, Kayla.

* * *

"Girl, what's up? Where you been at? You act like you can't call a sistah!" Kayla said to me, as soon as she picked up her phone.

Kayla Ricks was from the Southside of D.C. like Rashard. She's the loud ghetto type, who speaks her mind and doesn't care whose feelings she hurts. She's a rare brown color, with shoulder length hair that she keeps dyed different colors. She's about 5'6, probably a little bigger than me. It has been said that we look alike, but I don't believe so. Kayla cheers with Force Spirit too. She's an awesome cheerleader, but sometimes I don't understand how she can get things accomplished with her ghetto and playful personality.

I met her when I was three and first began cheering. She

was the only one in the group my age, everybody else was four and five and always called us the babies, so we just started hanging together. The reason I cherish her as one of my best friends is because she's always there when I need someone to lean on.

"Girl, guess what happened to me today?" I said, excitedly.

"What?"

"I was on my way to third period when I ran into Shard, and you know I don't usually see him until after school. Anyway, he called me over and slobbered me down right there in the hallway in front of everyone."

"Girl, stop lying!" Kayla screamed.

"I'm not lying, I'm so serious! We kissed again briefly after school!"

"Was it good?" Kayla asked, curious to know.

"Girl! That joint had me feeling good all over."

"Kourtney, is your homework done," Terry yelled from downstairs.

"Uh….. gotta go. I'll just see you at practice tonight," I said, sort of annoyed at having our conversation cut short.

"A'ight, see you later," she laughed.

* * *

At practice, Coach Laneen gave us the biggest speech of all times. She told us this would be our last practice before the competition, and since we were a senior advance all-star team, she expected us to perfect our stunts, tighten our motions, and give up cheering facials at all times.

Coach Laneen Black was serious when it came to cheerleading. She was always saying, "Attitude and confidence is everything and if you carry a nasty attitude, nothing will get accomplished. Your attitude determines your altitude," was her favorite line. It was even plastered on the entrance of the gym door. Not only was she the coach for us older girls, but she was also a certified judge. Coach Laneen didn't play when it came to cheering. I believed she put nothing before cheering.

"Alright girls, let's get ready for practice!" Coach Laneen yelled. She blew her whistle and began the count "5, 6, 7, 8, Set 1, 2, toss, 3, 4, cradle, 5, 6, hold, 7, 8, move, 1, 2, stop!

She took us through a rigorous practice for thirty minutes straight before allowing us to break.

"Okay, take 15 minutes," she yelled.

"Ah, Kourtney, where you going tonight?" Kayla asked, as we sat on the mat trying to catch our breath.

"Home, why?" I asked.

"'Cause I was thinking maybe I could come over for the weekend and we could hang out?"

"Yeah, I guess you can come over," I said.

"Me too, right?" another cheerleader asked.

"A'ight, I'll have to ask my mom. Who's all coming over?"

"Girl, the whole clique," Kayla answered.

"A'ight," I said. Before I could get to my cell phone, I spotted Stef strut past from the corner of my eye. She rolled her eyes at me for no apparent reason. Hearing Coach Laneen's voice kept me from stepping to Ms. Stef. *But she had one coming. Practice first*, I thought as I set for the opening cheer, with a smirk on my face.

* * *

As I was putting my pants on after practice, my cell phone began to blast. When I heard *"Started When We Were Younger, You Were My Boo"* ring tone, I knew who was calling. It was my one and only, Rashard.

"Hey, did your mom tell you I'm picking you up from

practice?"

"No, she didn't. But I'm getting ready to call her because Meka and the girls wanna come over."

"That's my girl. Always the center of attention."

"I'll be there soon. You know I love you," he said, before hanging up.

"Right, Shard," I retorted, as I hung up the phone.

I called home to ask my mom if the girls could come over for the weekend. She said she didn't care as long as everyone was on their best behavior. Also, she said she expected us to go to bed early since we had a competition in the morning. Competitions to her were like preparing for the SAT.

"A'ight," I said. I couldn't believe how serious she was.

After hanging up, I turned around to see all the girls looking nervously at me to see what my mom had said. Our place was small but everybody wanted to hang at my house. Before I knew it, five girls were lined up at the door waiting for Rashard to come; Jameka, Kristle, Maleka, Kayla, and Bre.

When Rashard pulled up all of us ran out to hop in his father's truck.

"Where they going?" he asked.

"I need you to take my girls to their houses so they can get some clothes for the weekend."

"Umm…" Rashard said, not really wanting to do this, but knowing he wouldn't be able to say no.

"Please," I begged.

"Okay, but only for you. You better be glad I have my father's truck." He smiled at me.

I shot him a fake smile right back.

* * *

After picking up everybody's clothes, we all went to

Denny's. In the restaurant, Rashard kept sucking on my neck, causing my hormones to rage. I had never had sex before, but right then and there I felt like I had. Rashard started whispering little freaky stuff in my ear, until he noticed a young girl about my age wearing some fancy shades. She was surrounded by four guys that resembled burly bodyguards. His attention was now completely focused on her.

"You want her?" I asked.

"No. I want you. Do you want me?"

"Yeah." I smiled. His attention was back on me.

"Do you love me?" he asked, while kissing my neck.

I answered quickly, knowing that I was saying the right thing. "No and stop asking me that."

He stopped kissing on my neck. Shocked, he stuttered, "Fine, I won't ask you again."

"Yes, Shard, I love you but I'm just scared."

"Scared of what?"

By now everyone was staring and Bre was sitting with her hand on her heart. I became embarrassed because I suddenly realized that everyone was listening to us.

"Bre, what are you doing?" I asked.

"Nothing, this is just so beautiful."

"Girl, you're so dramatic. You need to be an actress on HBO or SHOWTIME 'cause you trippin'," Kayla said.

"Right, and don't forget *nosey*," I said. I pulled Rashard up from his seat so that we could move to another booth to have a little more privacy.

After sitting at a booth far away from them, Rashard questioned me like an inmate on trial. "What are you scared of? I would never hurt you ever. You mean the world to me."

"Honestly, Shard, I don't love you. I was just so tired of you asking me. I didn't want to hurt your feelings. So please stop asking me and let me say it when I'm ready. Besides, I have too much on my mind these days. I don't want to lose focus on the upcoming cheerleading competition. You know cheerleading is my life. I don't need any confusion right now. Besides, you need to say on top of your game so the scouts will continue to look at you this season."

"You should be worried about me looking at you this season." His tone had changed completely. "I do have needs!"

Out of nowhere I asked, "Shard, are you tryna rush me into something that I'm not thinking about right now. I need to go to college."

"Me too," he said. "I don't wanna be the only guy in college wishing I had been with my woman.

"So, this explains why you're rushing everything." It got really quiet. "Listen, Shard, you don't have to rush nothing. I'll still be here when you get back from college."

"You promise to always be true?" he asked as he tilted my chin up. He gave me full eye contact. And keep your stock up."

I laughed. "Yes, Shard, now stop trippin'." I tried to lighten the mood.

I'm ready to go home 'cause we have a long day tomorrow. You'll be there, right?"

"Kourtney, you know I love seeing my girl in the spotlight. That's why folks sweat me so bad. I always got the hottest chick." He smiled.

I felt like anybody who wanted to be with me would have to be able to support me by showing up at my competitions. But Rashard was a show-off. I knew he'd be there just so he could ride off my fame at the arena. As usual, he'd watch my spectacular performance and brag about me for weeks to his boys.

* * *

"Get up now! It's 8:30! If y'all hadn't stayed up late, y'all wouldn't have a problem getting up this morning," my mom said coming into my bedroom. She was quite annoyed that we were still asleep when we had to meet our team at 10:30. "Who's getting in the shower first?" she asked, cutting my light on.

Within minutes everyone was getting ready. I ran downstairs to see if my mother needed any help with breakfast. "So, don't you think you're spending a little too much time with Rashard?" my mom asked bluntly.

"Not really."

She shook her head. "You think it's cute. Never focus all of your attention on some boy." She shook her finger at me like I was being grounded. "You need to make sure your life is in order, then worry about Rashard. I bet when it comes to you or what he has to do, you'll be put on the back burner. Besides, it seems to me that Rashard only wants you because you're popular. You're a showpiece for him."

My lip dropped. "That's not true," I said defending him. "He likes me because I'm real." I tried to get my mother to understand.

"Okay………," she finally said. Everything you're going through as a teenager, I've been there. I can see things clearer than you. It's my job to warn you!"

"Okay, Mommy. If that's what you want to believe. I mean, you don't have to like Rashard but don't blame him for something that's not true."

"Kourtney, I do like Rashard. I'm just talking about life and how things happen." She walked over and tapped me on the knee on her way out the kitchen.

"Okay, Mommy, I got ya," I replied.

She yelled to the girls upstairs. "Are you girls almost ready to leave? You know I have to be there early to meet the youth teams."

"Can I drive the truck? There's not enough room in the car for all of us and our bags," I said.

"That's fine, but be careful, and no stopping anywhere," she said heading out the door.

* * *

We arrived at the Showplace Arena at 10:15a.m. *Here we go again*, were my thoughts as we entered the Arena. We could feel the looks, the attention and hear the whispers we always tended to get from our local competitive teams. As we walked toward our team, I noticed a girl named Mahogany from the Firehawks' team. She watched my every move like I had stolen something from her. I smacked my lips and kept on walking. *This rivalry thing is going way too far*, I thought.

"By the time we met with our team Coach Laneen was well into one of her speeches. "Okay girls, let's show them the true ladies and champions we are. Represent with grace and pride," she said, giving us her last minute pep talk.

"Yeah, you know how we do it on the floor," Maleka said, with a huge smile on her face. Kristle and our smashing set of twin tumblers slapped high fives and giggled the whole time. They loved all of the attention.

Force Spirit took the regional competition with our youth teams. They were on fire and we cheered them on as loud as we could. Our coaches were pumped and so were all the cheerleaders in the organization. Fifteen minutes before it was time for my team to report to the practice mat, I spotted Rashard and his crew in the stands. From that moment on, I had goose bumps.

"Kourtney, go get your teammates together so that we can go to the practice mat. But before we do, I need to talk to the team," Coach Laneen said.

"We could probably give the speech she's about to give us,"

Bre said, laughing.

"Yeah, we've heard it over and over again for ten years," Kayla said, with a giggle.

"Kourtney, I know you aren't talking while I'm talking," Coach Neen said, not realizing it was the other girls causing the chatter.

"Oh, my God, why are you always accusing me of talking?" I asked? I pretended to be hurt and tried to make my coach laugh as well as stop the butterflies in my stomach.

Suddenly, I felt someone put their hands over my eyes and whisper, "Who's the best flyer in the world?"

To my surprise it was Keya. Keya was a former Force Spirit cheerleader, who was in her freshman year of college, cheering for Georgia Tech on a full scholarship. She was my girl. When we were teammates, she helped me to get my skills down pat.

When I turned around to hug her, all my nervous jitters disappeared. As I looked around at all the girls, I realized why we were the reigning National Champions for three years straight. I knew from that moment we owned the floor. Our former teammate gave us a pep talk and we all prayed together.

The announcer called our team name and we took to the mat. We approached the performance with all the confidence and support we needed. As I stood on the mat, I looked up to where Rashard was sitting. I tried to get his attention, but couldn't. It didn't surprise me that he was really into the competition. I thought to myself, *he better not be zooming in on another girl*. I turned to look at the Force Spirit coaching staff standing near the speaker, and as my eyes met my mom's, she gave me a wink and a thumb's up. From that point on, I was in my zone. Every tumbling pass that was thrown was completed, we had no missed stunts or bobbles; we worked that routine. I could barely hear the music because the crowd appeal was so loud. The routine was simply flawless. Once again, we had torn the floor up.

As I walked off the floor, a woman approached me. She complimented me on our great performance. She was the Assistant Cheerleading Coach for the University of Miami, my dream school. She asked me if we would be attending the nationals because her Head Coach would be there scouting and she wanted to recommend me as a candidate for a scholarship. She said they were looking for another flyer and someone to base their cheerleading squad. She gave me her card. I thanked her and she walked off.

As the Firehawk's prepared to take the floor, I decided not to watch their performance. It was a ritual for our team to watch them together. After all, they were our challengers. I ran over to my mother and jumped on her, hugging her neck tightly. As I told her about the conversation I had with Ms. Ross from the University of Miami, the Firehawks' chants got louder and louder. My mom had tears in her eyes when she told me how proud she was of me. As we embraced again we both noticed that the crowd was going crazy. It was like being at a Redskins playoff game. "We're #1!" they chanted. "We're #1." I even wanted to chant.

I looked over at my team members as they watched the Firehawks intensely. At this point Mahogany was really connecting with the crowd. As the funky hip hop music began she immediately hit a triple, backwards flip, at high speed across the floor. She was really doing her thing, and *well* I might add. I couldn't watch the Firehawks show us up any longer. I looked toward Rashard who was standing on his feet watching Mahogany like a hawk. I was devastated.

* * *

After the competition and awards ceremony, the entire squad decided to go out to eat to celebrate. I declined. When we came out of the locker room, I got my phone out to call Rashard to see where his butt went. I called him but there was no answer. I had a funny feeling, 'cause he always answered my call.

After about ten more minutes of small talk with the girls, my phone rang. I knew exactly who it was. "Where are you and why did you leave?" I said angrily.

"I had to go somewhere."

"Where?"

"My sister called and asked me to go to the store for her."

"So, you're telling me your sister couldn't wait?

"Because I didn't want…"

"Yeah, whatever Shard. I'll talk to you when I talk to you. Goodbye!" I said, as I hung up the phone in his ear.

"Don't let him get in your head. You just won grand champion. Come on, let's roll," Kayla said, as she picked up my bag.

* * *

"Hey Kourtney, the half time show yesterday was the bomb. You really did your thang on that floor," Mark, a boy from the track team said. He liked me a lot. That was the good thing about cheering at school as opposed to cheering for Force Spirit- the all star team. *I get more interaction with the boys.*

"Thanks," I said with a half smile on my face. I tried to hurry so Rashard wouldn't think I was cheating on him.

As I sat in my English class, I couldn't help but think about how close Rashard and I had gotten over the last few months. Ever since I chastised him about leaving the competition, he's been so sweet. I haven't had to catch the school bus home and he's insisted on driving me back and forth to both school and all star cheerleading practice.

"Earth to Kourtney," Maleka said at the end of class, in a sarcastic tone. "Are you going to tumbling after the game this evening? You know if we miss practice Coach Neen is gonna be hot with us."

"Shoot, I forgot. I told Shard I was going with him to the movies after the game. I guess I'm gonna have to tell him I can't go now. I have to work on my new tumbling pass," I said.

"Yeah, you betta. You know you missed the last two practices, bunnin' up with Shard," Maleka said.

Here we go. "I got this and let's not talk about being bunned up," I said defending myself, as I was walking to my locker.

"Whatever. Hey, when are you going to have another girl's night? We haven't hung out in over a month."

"Maybe we can do it this weekend since we have to do that special performance on Saturday."

"Okay. I'll ask my mother," I told her, walking away. "Rashard, can I talk to you for a minute?" I said. I walked up to his locker where he was chillin' with his boys.

"What's up?" he asked, as he leaned on his locker.

"I can't go with you to the movies this evening. I forgot that we have all star practice after the game today."

"Kourt, I was really looking forward to being with you. You can't miss what, one practice?" He pulled me towards him. He kissed my lips softly. He really knew how to make me tingle.

"I've missed two practices already, but I'll see what I can do. I'm going to get dressed for the game."

"Shard, I thought you said your lady would do anything for you," Black asked, as I was walking away.

"She will," he replied softly.

He obviously didn't think that I heard him. I started to go off, but decided against it. I didn't want to throw him off of his game. The basketball game was scheduled to start in twenty minutes. As usual, it was intense. Rashard was on the floor doing his thing and I held down the sidelines.

"During the time out, we're going over to do the friendship circle with the other team cheerleaders," I told the other cheerleaders.

Five minutes later, the whistle blew to let us know it was time. As they approached the middle of the court, Kourtney began to talk. "Hi, I'm Kourtney, the captain. This is Maleka, she's the co-captain." Maleka flashed a half smile.

"I'm Megan, and this is Shantel, we're the captains also," she said, in a don't even try it tone.

Both teams formed a circle and did their jumps and tumble passes, trying to outdo the other team. When it got down to the two captains, it was like being at competition. By then, the basketball teams were ready to take the floor. They looked on as we took this time to show off our skills. Megan looked over and saw Rashard standing there; she winked her eye. Then Megan and Shantel threw double toe backs in sequence. Maleka and I winked without speaking and we both knew it was on. As we set up for our tumbling pass, the whistle blew. *We didn't care.* We showed off ending with a layout and a twist. The spectators cheered!

Rashard stood there, proud that his girl knew how to hold her own. He looked up at the girl that had winked at him and mouthed, *pick your face up.*

At the end of the game, when Rashard got to his car he noticed a note on his windshield. It read: *Congratulations on your win! I like your doggy style. Give me a call at 240-568-0939. You know who.* Rashard folded the note up and put it in his glove compartment.

* * *

"Kourtney, we need to talk," my mom said, when I came into the house.

"What is it Mom? I have a test to study for."

"You're spending too much time with Rashard. You missed tumbling practice twice already. You need to get focused and stop letting that fast little boy and his hormones get to you."

"Mommy, I made it to practice today after the game. I'm not losing focus, you're just overreacting. *Gosh, why won't she leave me alone? She's always nagging me. Little does she know Shard loves me and I love him,* I said to myself. I refused to let her know that I left practice early today, because if I did, she'd have a fit.

"Don't you know that all he wants is one thing from you? Are you willing to throw away everything you have worked hard for, for him?"

"Okay Ma, you're right. I'll stay focused. I'm also gonna do my tape and send it to Ms. Ross this weekend.

* * *

I woke up to my phone ringing in the middle of the night. I looked at the clock and it read 1:30 am.

"Hello," I said, half awake.

"Hey baby, are you asleep?" Rashard asked.

"Yes, I am," I snapped. Even though I was happy to hear his voice, I needed my rest.

"I called to say I love you."

"I love you too," I said. But I have to get some sleep. I have to get my tape together to send to this recruiter."

"What recruiter?"

"If you hadn't skipped out, you would've known she came to see me at the competition."

"That's good. Get some rest and I'll talk to you tomorrow,"

he said, thinking that he had hung up the phone.

Just then, I thought I heard a female's voice coming from his phone. "Didn't I tell you to be quiet while I'm on the phone with my girl!" He snapped at the anonymous female in his car, never realizing that he hadn't hung up his phone. *I must be tired, Shard loves me and wouldn't cheat on me*, I thought as I fell back to sleep.

* * *

When I arrived at the gym, my stunt group was already ready to practice.

"You're late Ms. Kourtney," Maleka said, as she sat on the mat in a straddle position.

"Sorry, are y'all ready to start?"

"Come on y'all, we need to be finished before the Junior Preps come in for practice.

We nailed our routine after three tries. We were given an hour break before our next practice session was scheduled to begin. As we rushed out the door, Coach Neen yelled, "Girls, be back here on time for practice and I'm not playing!"

I called Rashard from my cell phone, hoping to see him before I was due back at the gym. He answered his phone on the first ring.

"Hey boo, what's up?" he said.

"Where are you? I have a free hour and I want to see you."

"I'm in the house, come on over."

"If my mom lets me use her car, I'll be on my way," I said. I located my mom in the gym talking with Coach Neen. "Mom, can I use your car to make a quick run?" I asked her.

"A run to where Kourtney?" she said, knowing already where I wanted to go.

"I wanna run and yell at Shard before our next practice,"

"Okay, but you better have your butt back here on time," she said, handing me her car keys.

"Thanks Mom, love ya," I said, running out of the gym.

While driving to Rashard's, I thought to myself, *I hope he doesn't start with that love stuff today.*

"Hello Kourtney," Ms. Smith, Rashard's mom said, opening the door.

"Hello Ms. Smith, is Rashard home?"

"Sure, he's in the basement looking at TV. Go on down."

"Okay, thanks."

"Hey baby," Rashard said, pulling me near him for a kiss.

I sat down on the sofa next to him and started looking at the movie that he was watching. I started thinking about the voice I heard on the phone, so I said, "Shard, who was in the car with you last night?"

"Nobody," he replied, never even looking my way. "Why?"

"I thought I heard someone in the car with you," I said, not really believing his answer.

"If you stop faking and treat me like your man, you wouldn't be hearing voices. You know that's your mind playing tricks on you because you keep holding out on me."

"Shard, I thought we went over this before. If you keep on pressuring me, I'm leaving," I said, standing up.

"Okay, I'ma chill. Don't leave. I like having you around." He pulled me down on the sofa and looked me in my eyes. "Kourtney Taylor, I love you." We began to kiss.

Maybe he's right. Maybe I should give him some before he goes to college before someone else does, I thought, lying in his arms as we dozed off.

* * *

When I pulled into the parking space, I realized I was

running late. I hurried into the gym and started stretching. I couldn't get Rashard off my mind.

"Earth to Kourtney. Where's your mind?" Kayla said, as she grabbed my hand and pulled me to my feet.

"I was just daydreaming."

"I can see that. Did you hear what we're doing?"

"Yeah, set 5, 6, 7, 8."

"Kourt, what's wrong?" Maleka said. "Get it together."

"Maybe it's the hickey on her neck that's stopping her," Kayla said, with a grin on her face.

"Stop playing," I said running to the bathroom, with all the girls right behind me. "My mother's gonna kill me!" I looked in the mirror to see the hickey.

"It's not that bad," Kayla said, as she looked in the mirror.

"I can hear her now, 'Oh, so you gonna let that fast boy have his way with you, huh?'"

"You need to tell her and don't try to hide it," Maleka said, pushing my head over to get a better look. "You don't want to mess up the trust that you and her have."

Coach Neen came into the bathroom. "Ladies, is this cheerleading practice or social hour? We have nationals to prepare for. Let me see the tumble run. Kourtney, I need for you to work on your twist. Do you need a spotter?"

"No, I don't. I got it," I said.

"I'll spot you personally?" she said.

"I got this, trust me," I said, with a smirk on my face.

Okay, Kourtney, snap out of it, you can do this. Those were my last thoughts as I ran out of the corner on my count.

*　*　*

"She's awake," the young nurse said. "Kourtney, can you hear me?" she asked me.

"Yes I can. Why are you yelling and where am I?"

"You're in Southern Maryland Hospital," my mother said.

"You were hurt at practice. You lost control of your twist and hit the wall."

"You obtained a head injury," the nurse said.

"Kourtney, do you know what today is?" my father asked.

"Yes, it's Sunday," I said. "How did you get here Daddy?"

"No baby, it's Tuesday not Sunday. I arrived Sunday night."

"I'm going to take her down for some x-rays. You all can wait here if you like," the nurse said, as she unplugged my IV.

"Where did all of those balloons come from?" I asked, as she pushed me into the hall.

"Your friends. They're in the waiting room. They've been here day in and day out. They can come in and visit for a little while when you get back."

I wondered if Shard had been crying his eyes out over my accident. *I know he was scared when he saw me this way*, I thought as I closed my eyes and enjoyed the ride.

"Okay, Ms Kourtney, you seem to be recovering well from your injuries, but I'm afraid you'll have to stay here until further notice. I'll take you back up to your room and I want you to make sure you get some rest," the nurse said.

"Will I be able to cheer again?" I asked the nurse.

"I'm sure you will, you just have to take it easy for a while. You may not be able to flip right away, but that's something you need to discuss with your doctor."

When I got back to my room, everybody from my team was there; Maleka, Jameka, Kristle, Mi Mi, and Keya. They started explaining how they all had burst out crying when I hit the wall.

"So, did anybody talk to Shard?" I asked, out of curiosity.

"Well, I told him what was going on but he didn't sound like he cared much," Kayla stated, as she walked through the door with more balloons.

"That's crazy, I know he cares about me. Why would you even say that Kayla?" I asked, getting really worked up.

"Well, Kourt, when I told him all he said was okay and to tell you that he hopes you feel better, and to call him when you get a chance. I asked him if he was coming to come see you. All he kept saying was tell you to call him when you get a chance."

I looked at her as if she was lying. My mother was even shocked. I picked up the hospital phone and called his cell phone.

"Hello," an unfamiliar female voice said, answering his phone.

Instantly my heart dropped. "Hello, can I speak to Rashard please?"

"May I ask who's calling?"

"This is Kourtney. May I ask whom I'm speaking with?" I retorted. By now everyone in the room was staring at me.

"Yes, this is Mahogany. Here is Rashard, hold on." I waited anxiously until Rashard finally came to the phone.

"Hello," Rashard said.

"Where are you? And why is that hood rat answering your phone?"

"Oh, Mahogany, she's just a friend. I'm at my house chillin'. What's up?"

"What? I'm here laid up in a hospital bed with a severe injury to my head and you at home chillin' with some little hoe. You tell me what's up?" I said.

"Look Kourt, I don't have time to play these games with you. It's not my fault you got broke cheering. I'm chillin' with my friend and don't feel the need to explain my actions to you. You know I'm focusing on getting ready for college!" he fired back.

"Yeah, you right, I know where you got to be and I know where I need to be. I'll call you back when I feel like it or when

I feel like you care." I was heartbroken.

"Kourt, I hope you feel better. Give me a call when you're ready to be a real woman," he said.

It felt like someone had reached in and snatched my heart out of my chest. "Oh, so it's like that," I said to Rashard. Click was the sound of the phone as I hung it up in his ear and burst into tears.

"Now baby, listen, I don't want you to get worked up about this boy, he's nothing. You need to focus on your health. What did the nurse say?" my mom asked, with a look of sympathy on her face.

"She just said that I'm recovering well, but I still have more tests and that I have to stay here until further notice."

"Well, I guess we'll leave now and come back tomorrow. We'll let you get a little more rest," Coach Neen directed everybody out.

"A'ight, Kourt. I'm going to go back to the hotel and get some rest. I'll be back first thing in the morning," my dad said, while kissing me on my forehead.

"Okay, Daddy, call me when you get there."

"Okay, baby. I love you," he said.

"I love you too," I stated back to him.

"Close your eyes," my mom stated rubbing my forehead. Instantly, I dozed back off to sleep.

* * *

When I woke up, I saw my Dad standing at the window on a business call. I just watched him as he handled his business over the phone. When he saw me looking at him, he quickly ended his conversation.

"Hey there squirt. How you holding up?" he said, coming over to the bed.

"I'm okay." *At least this accident gave me a chance to be closer to my father*, I thought. *Lately, we hadn't spent much time together at all.* I smiled as I looked at him. He took a quick step back as the nurse came to put more pain medicine through my IV.

"Dad, this is all my fault. I should've just let the coach spot me and I wouldn't have this problem," I said. I felt guilty for my actions.

"Now, just wait a minute. I'm not gonna let you sit here and blame yourself for something that was an accident. Now come on baby, we all make mistakes. We just have to learn from them. But I promise you'll get into your school of choice even if I have to sell my store."

"Thanks Dad, you're the best," I said. I reached up and hugged him. I closed my eyes and thought about the cold conversation I had with Rashard. I replayed the events over the last six months, silently crying as I drifted back off to sleep.

The entire week, my clique and family took turns keeping me company while I was in the hospital. That still didn't stop my mind from wondering and wanting to see Rashard. But I knew I needed to focus all of my strength on getting strong so that I'd be able to compete in the nationals, which were in three weeks. Despite what everyone thought, I was gonna be ready.

*   *   *

"Okay, Ms. Taylor, it seems you're recovering better than we thought. I have your release papers ready. You'll be released tomorrow morning at 9 o'clock," the nurse said, checking my chart.

"Thank you. I'm really tired of being in this place."

"Right now, I'm gonna take you down for one more round of tests," the nurse said, wheeling me out of the room.

When I got back to my room, it was about quarter after eleven. When I turned my cell phone on, I had over 22 messages. I called my voice mail from the hospital phone.

"Hey, Kourtney, this is Mi-Mi, call me asap. I have some news for you."

"Kourtney, this is your Mama. Call me when you get a chance. I love you."

"Kourtney, this is Kayla. Call me later, girl."

"Hey girl, this is Bre. Call me when you get this message, peace."

I ended the mailbox right there because I was already overwhelmed. Thinking about getting back into the swing of things had me stressed out. I closed my eyes and waited for the morning.

"I'm putting her on bed rest for approximately seven days. She's not to begin cheering or any kind of busy movement until after her check up," the doctor told my mother.

"So, basically doctor, you're saying you won't know when she can continue flipping or cheering until after her check up."

"Yes. Her check up is scheduled for Thursday, April 5th. I'll keep in touch to see how she's doing."

"Thank you doctor."

"Johnson, Dr. Johnson. You're quite welcome," the doctor stated, as we departed the hospital.

When I got home, my mother made sure I was in the house lounging or sleeping every day. I was so bored, I wanted to go back to school and get back to practice.

"Mommy, please let me go back to school tomorrow. If I can't last all day I promise I'll call you so you can come pick me up," I begged my mother one evening.

My mother kept cooking dinner. She was thinking about how seeing Rashard might affect me. She thought I was doing well, but noticed my sadness at times. But at the same time, she had to face the facts and it just might do me good to be at school.

"Okay, but if you start to feel weak or lightheaded, you better call me. Baby, you need to realize that Rashard losing you is his loss, not yours."

"I know Mommy, and I promise I'll call you." I ran upstairs. *I should call the girls and let them now I'm coming back to school. Nah, I'll surprise them.* I started getting my clothes together for the next day, I had to be fresh on my return.

* * *

"Kourtney!!!!" Bre, Maleka and Jontice yelled in unison, running to my locker.

"What are you doing back? I thought you weren't due back until Monday?" Jontice said, taking my books out of my arms.

"My mother let me come back. But I had to promise her that if I start to feel bad I'd call her to come get me."

"Kourt, you know Shard is back, and ever since he's been back, he's been talking to Stef. I'm only telling you because I didn't want you to be in shock when you saw them together," Maleka said, looking to see if I was gonna break down.

"Girl, I have to worry about being strong so I can do me at the nationals. Later for that loser, and as for Stef, she can just keep doing her."

"That's so foul," Bre said, shaking her head.

"I know that's right," Jontice said, as they walked off.

After school, as I was walking down the hall, I saw a group of boys standing on the Green Hall.

"Hey Kourt, I heard about your accident. I see you're still looking good," Black said flirting.

"Always. How are you Shard?" I asked, in a cheerful voice.

"Hey," he said, sounding dry.

With a big grin on my face, I walked away from the group and headed toward the front of the school to meet my mother out front. I felt good that I didn't give in to Rashard, but at the same time, I felt a sense of sadness.

* * *

With a clean bill of health and one week to practice for the nationals, I was able to return to practice.

"Hello, Kourtney. I see you're early and ready to practice," Coach Laneen said, placing her hand on my shoulder.

"Yes," I said, smiling from ear to ear. "Do you think I can get some private tumbling lessons in this week?"

"Look, Kourt, I don't want you to overdo it. I don't want you to push yourself. Do what's comfortable for you."

"Coach Neen, I've never been more ready for anything in my life. I'm totally focused and confident. This is my destiny."

"I hear you. I'll let you know the times that are available at the end of practice. Go to the opening," she said, as she walked on the mat.

I practiced as if I'd never missed a beat. I was right at home on that mat. My sadness was gone because this is what made me complete.

At the end of practice, Coach Laneen said, "Good practice ladies. Don't forget to go and check the team announcements. Kourtney, welcome back."

"Kourtney, can I talk to you a minute?" Stef said, as we were walking to the showers.

"Sure, Stef, what's up?"

"I just want you to know that I'm glad you're better. We're on the same team and I don't want any hard feelings between us. I want you to know I wasn't talking to Shard when the two of you were together. But now, we're in love," Stef said, with her head down.

I had mixed emotions over Stef's announcement. I wanted to slap the taste out of her mouth, but at the same time, I thought it was funny how things happen.

With a grin on my face, I was determined to be the bigger person, so I responded, "Look, Stef, it doesn't matter to me. That's your thing. I have enough on my mind other than worrying about you and Shard. Do you sweetie, and Stef, be careful. Once a dog always a dog."

I walked out the gym, leaving Stef standing there waiting for her ride. Leaving the parking lot, I passed Rashard. I had to laugh to keep from crying.

I trained hard and wasn't late for a single practice or tumbling session. I stayed to myself all week. My focus changed from boys and hanging with friends to my studies and cheering.

* * *

When we arrived at the Patriot Center, most of the girls were already there.

"I love the nationals, all the glitz and glamour is so exciting," I said.

"Where are we sitting?" Kayla asked.

"Go through Gate 5, you should see them over there," a member of the coaching staff said.

"Thanks." We went to find our seats.

Everybody was doing their thing; eating, doing hair, and talking on their phones. I asked Kayla to walk around with me so I could see if Ms. Ross and the head coach that were there to look at my performance. There were hundreds of teams and spectators in attendance. I had no success of finding her. When we returned to our seats, Coach Neen came and told us we needed to start getting ready.

On the practice mat, we nailed the stunts, dances and cheers. When we got to the tumble run, I froze. I couldn't get myself together. Every time it was my turn, I'd get a funny feeling in the pit of my stomach. I kept thinking back to my accident.

"Come on, Kourtney, you can do it," Meka said, patting me on my back.

As we walked to the deck to await our turn, I forced a smile on my face, put my head down and closed my eyes. I could see my mother. She told me to be proud of my strength and to trust in God. Stay focused, she mouthed.

The background lights dimmed, spotlights flashed and the announcer said, "Welcome to the floor Force Spirit All-Starssssssss!!!!"

As I set in my position, I looked in the stands to my right. To my surprise, there was Ms. Ross and the Recruiter sitting in the stands watching with notepads out. When I looked up two rows, there was Rashard smiling and winking at me. He mouthed, *you got this*. I quickly turned away. I spotted my mother; she mouthed, *I love you*. The music started and I was in my zone. When I went to my corner to perform my tumbling pass, I could feel the confidence come over me. My number came and I ran out. I did what I had been practicing all week. When I landed the crowd went wild.

WORDS FROM
THE AUTHORS

Teenagers, we hope the stories in this book have been a wake up call!

Please log onto www.lifechangingbooks.net and go to the Teenage Bluez link to vote for your favorite story in the Message Board. We really want to hear your comments.

CALL FOR
STORY SUBMISSIONS

We're now accepting all ideas/submissions for short stories to be included in Teenage Bluez – Series #2. All submissions must be at least 20 pages, but no longer than 30 pages. Stories submitted must not contain any profanity or explicit sex scenes. Teenage male authors are encouraged. All submissions must deal with today's teenage issues, such as, but not limited to: Peer Pressure, Drugs, Sports, Parents and Teen Relationships.

Submit all stories to www.lifechangingbooks.net.

or
Life Changing Books
PO Box 423
Brandywine, MD 20613

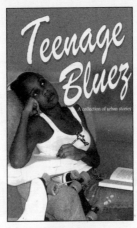

$10.99

Maryland residens, please add 5% sales tax.
+ Shipping/handling$3.50 (U.S. Priority Mail)

Make check or money order payable to:
Life Changing Books
(please do not send cash)

Life Changing Books
PO Box 423, Brandywine, MD 20613

Purchaser information: (please print)

Name_____

Address_____

City_____

State and Zip_____

Number of books requested   _____

Total for this order $_____

Additional copies may also be ordered online at
<u>www.lifechangingbooks.net</u>

TEENAGE BLUEZ SERIES II

COMING SOON!!!!

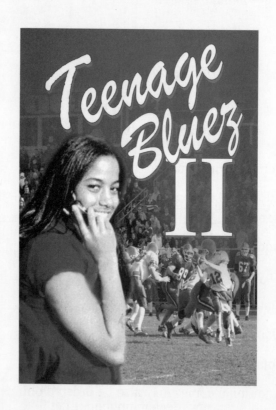

Fourteen year old Dymond is at a pivotal point in her life... high school. Not only is she faced with the challenges of being a freshman, but also from members in her crew - Kera and Porsha. Both of them have boyfriends however; Dymond has yet to find one. Well, that is until she met Kyle Banks.

Dymond finds herself falling face first nose wide open for him. Even lying to her mother (with the help of her girls) to be with him, but how many lies can you tell before it catches up to you? Ms. Dymond In The Rough will soon find out!

Dymond In The Rough - now available!
(10 - 16 years age group)